MEN
in
UNIFORM

Courteous, courageous and commanding—
these heroes lay it all on the line for the
people they love in more than fifty stories about
loyalty, bravery and romance.
Don't miss a single one!

VALERIE PARV

CODE NAME: PRINCE

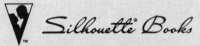

Published by Silhouette Books

America's Publisher of Contemporary Romance

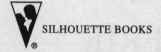

SILHOUETTE BOOKS

ISBN-13: 978-0-373-36272-1

CODE NAME: PRINCE

Recycling programs
for this product may
not exist in your area.

VALERIE PARV

With 25 million copies of her books sold internationally, including many Waldenbooks bestsellers, it's no wonder Valerie Parv is known as Australia's queen of romance and is the recognized media spokesperson for all things romantic.

Valerie lives in Australia's capital city of Canberra, where she is a volunteer zoo guide. She draws on this and other aspects of her life for many of her novels, having spent almost thirty-eight years happily married to her romantic hero, Paul. As she says, "Love gives you wings—romance helps you fly."

To Sandy, Barry and Phyllis
with love and thanks for your friendship and support.

Chapter One

Ben Lockhart's first waking thought was how much he would like to get his hands on whoever was using a jackhammer inside his head. He opened his eyes then snapped them shut again. Letting the light in was a really bad idea. So was moving.

He made himself lie still and think. As a navy man he wasn't anybody's idea of an angel, but he could usually remember what he'd done to get this hungover, especially when the party was as spectacular as last night's must have been. Yet try as he might, he couldn't recall a single detail.

Then it came back to him. He couldn't remember the party because there hadn't been one. He had been doubling for his cousin, Prince Nicholas Stanbury,

Prince Regent; acting for the king of Edenbourg while King Michael was missing and believed kidnapped.

The pounding in Ben's head reminded him painfully that his last memory was of being dragged into a limousine that had infiltrated the royal cavalcade. Falling for the pretense that he was Prince Nicholas, his captors had blindfolded and bound him then injected him with a knockout drug, leaving him to wake up here, wherever here was.

Ben felt a frown start, wishing that his headache *had* been due to over-indulgence. It would have been easier to deal with than the task ahead of him. Now he had to find out who was behind these attacks on the royal family.

Easy enough if you said it quickly, Ben thought, wincing as movement sent a fresh wave of pain surging through his skull. What in the name of Edenbourg had they given him? He opened his eyes more cautiously, hoping he could get a look at his watch and try to work out how long he'd been unconscious, only to find his hands were securely tied to the white wrought-iron bedstead on which he lay. A battered teddy bear sat on the pillow beside his head.

Teddy bear? What sort of kidnappers kept a teddy bear? Ignoring the urge to close his eyes again, he waited until the room stopped spinning, then made himself take stock. He was lying on a diminutive bed. His feet overhung the end by a good six inches, the bed evidently being meant for someone a lot smaller than his six-foot frame.

Beside the bed stood a white-painted dresser. On it

sat a stuffed dog, a homemade rag doll and a water glass that made him lick his dry lips, wishing he could reach it. Above the dresser was a multi-paned window hung with dainty floral curtains that matched the frilled coverlet beneath him. On the opposite wall were two doors. One he presumed led to a closet and the other into the rest of the house. Right now, both doors were closed.

Twisting his body to try to see out the window and get an idea of where he was only resulted in making the rope bite deeper into his wrists, adding to his discomfort. He made himself lie still. His captors hadn't gone to this much trouble to let him die of starvation or thirst. Sooner or later somebody was bound to come in and check on him. Until then it made more sense to rest and let the drug work its way out of his system.

He didn't have long to wait.

After what he judged to be about half an hour he saw the china handle on one of the doors begin to turn. He closed his eyes and slowed his breathing with the idea of buying himself a few minutes to assess his captor.

He heard tentative footsteps on the polished wood floor as someone approached the bed, but the first thing that hit him was the scent of roses. It struck him as being as incongruous as the teddy bear. He was so startled that he almost opened his eyes to get a look at the source of the delicious scent teasing his nostrils like a breath of spring.

"I know you're awake."

The soft, musical voice so exactly matched the scent that another shock wave rippled through him, as well as something much more basic. He schooled himself to resist it. Obviously, his captor was a woman, but that didn't mean he had to react like a man. The problem seemed to be convincing his body. This time he did open his eyes, barely remembering to do it slowly to create the impression that he was only now coming around.

What met his eyes was so unexpected that he would have jerked upright if not for the ropes binding him to the bed. Leaning over him was the most beautiful woman he had ever seen. Tall and willowy, she had hair the color of ripe corn scattered with paler highlights, over eyes as blue as a summer sky. He saw that they were clouded now with something—fear? It seemed odd, given that he was the captive.

He reminded himself again that she was one of the kidnappers. Not one of those who had abducted and drugged him. If she had been, he knew he would have noticed her scent even as he was going under. So she hadn't been part of that scene. But she was here and despite the naked fear he read in her eyes, she made no move to untie him.

"How did you know I was awake?" he asked, hearing his voice rasp as an aftereffect of his rough treatment.

She heard it too, because she picked up the glass of water from the dresser and lifted it to his lips. With her free hand, she supported his head so he could drink. Her fingers felt like the caress of velvet against the back of his neck. When some of the water dribbled down his chin, she put the glass down long enough to brush the droplets away with the back of her hand. He felt a strong urge to capture those delicate fingers in his mouth.

What was he thinking? She was the enemy, remember? Probably chosen precisely because his captors expected her golden good looks to soften him up so he'd tell them whatever they needed to know. Well, to perdition with that idea. He'd tell them nothing. Nor would he think of her as an angel, when she was in league with whoever had captured him.

"Your eyelids were moving just the way Molly's do when she wants me to think she's asleep," the woman answered his question.

"And Molly is?"

She hesitated, then said, "My daughter."

Molly must be the child who normally slept in this room, he concluded. At the same time he wondered what kind of woman allowed her child to become involved in criminal activities.

He turned his head to one side and she took the hint, replacing the glass on the dresser. "Who are you?" he demanded.

The haunted look that had disappeared when he asked about Molly returned to her eyes, but he hardened his heart against it. "I can't tell you," she said in a voice barely above a whisper. Who was she afraid might hear her?

"At least tell me your first name." It came to him that he wanted to know as much to satisfy his own curiosity as to help his mission.

Her frightened glance flew to the door then back to him. "Meagan," she said. "You can call me Meagan."

"Meagan who?"

"I'm sorry, Your Highness, I mustn't say any more."

Her use of the title jarred him with its harsh reminder of his purpose. Of course, she thought he was Prince Nicholas, acting ruler of Edenbourg. "If you know who I am, you must know that what you're doing is high treason," he said in what he hoped was a royal tone of command.

She bit her full lower lip and he saw a mist spring to her eyes. "I'm aware of that, Your Highness."

He strained at the ropes. "Then release me at once."

She glanced over her shoulder as if to satisfy herself that the door was securely closed. "I can ease the bindings a little, but I dare not do more."

Why not? he wondered. For someone who was involved in the kidnapping of a prince, as she thought him to be, she didn't seem very sure of herself. In fact she seemed scared out of her wits. He caught himself before he murmured the words of reassurance that sprang to his lips, instead making his nod as imperious as if he truly were Prince Nicholas. "Anything would be an improvement on being trussed up like meat for the table."

Her fingers worried at the sturdy knots near his wrists. He was surprised to feel a rush of response as her cool touch whispered over his skin. "Is that better?" she asked in a barely audible tone.

As the strain on his arms eased fractionally, he released his breath in a relieved sigh. "Better would be untying me altogether, and telling me what's going on."

She shook her head, her hair falling in a silken

curtain around her face. Such delicate features, he thought. Such a beautiful mouth, mobile and generously shaped. As a man it disturbed him to see such beauty marred by distress, until he reminded himself that she had brought her troubles—whatever they were—on herself.

"I was only supposed to make sure you were awake, and offer you food if you're hungry. Are you?"

"Yes, now that you mention it." He wasn't, but he wanted to keep her in the room while he learned all he could from her. She turned to go and he said quickly, "How long was I unconscious?"

"Not long. They didn't want you to be harmed."

"They?"

"My…" She stopped herself. "I can't say any more."

He allowed a strangled breath to escape and saw her frown in concern.

"Are you ill or in pain?"

"Both, not surprisingly," he lied, knowing he should exploit her compassion while he had the chance. The notion felt uncomfortable, but he could see no other option. Now that the drug was wearing off, he felt his strength returning rapidly. The pain in his head was also fading, thank goodness. About the ache in his arms he could do nothing, so he ignored it. "Having you talk to me is taking my mind off how I feel," he said, not entirely untruthfully.

She chewed her full lower lip. "I suppose a few minutes longer won't hurt."

Just don't go, he urged inwardly. He told himself it

was because he needed information, but knew that the room would feel much more like a prison when she was no longer in it.

She looked panicky enough to flee if he said the wrong thing. "If you can't tell me where I am or why I was brought here, then tell me what the weather is like."

"The sun is out," she said carefully. "It's warm, and there's a light breeze blowing."

He had worked out all but the breeze for himself. "Are you always so literal?" he asked.

He had the satisfaction of seeing color seep into her cheeks. "You did ask about the weather."

"If I asked about you, would you answer as frankly?"

Her color deepened but she didn't look away. Courage as well as beauty, he concluded with a sense of gratification.

"Depends what you ask," she said.

He decided to try something harmless. "How old are you?"

Her lovely eyes widened, as if his question had caught her off guard. "Twenty-seven, why?"

"You look too innocent for twenty-seven. I'd have said no more than twenty."

He had expected her to be flattered. Most women were, if you underestimated their ages. Instead, she looked irritated. "I left innocence behind long ago, when I had Molly."

Reminded that she was probably married, since she had a child, he felt something like disappointment stab through him. Maybe she wasn't so innocent after all, even of her role in his kidnapping. He was usually a fairly good judge of character, but in this instance, it seemed he couldn't have been more wrong. "I suppose your husband is one of the kidnappers, and that's why you're involved," he said, hearing bitterness color his tone.

Her long lashes swept down over eyes he could swear had turned moist. "Molly's father is married to someone else."

"Then it's his loss."

Ben's sympathetic comment, made almost before he could prevent it, caught her by surprise. He saw it in the look she gave him.

"You're every bit as kind as I've read you were," she said.

Ben knew that his cousin's reputation hadn't always been entirely positive. For many years Prince Nicholas had been known as a playboy, until true love had tamed his wilder side. Now he was an exemplary husband and father, protector of the oppressed, and supporter of too many charitable causes to count.

Yes, Ben guessed, you could call his cousin kind. In his own way, Ben liked to think of himself as kind, too. Who didn't? But as a very minor royal with only one titled parent—his mother, Princess Karenna—he didn't get as much publicity as Nicholas. Ben would have hated it if he did, especially if his current ordeal was the reward one could expect for having a high profile.

The thought reminded Ben that as far as Meagan knew, he *was* Prince Nicholas. As such, he couldn't very well flirt with her to get her to tell him more, tempted though he was.

Tempted for a lot of reasons, not all to do with his situation, he realized to his chagrin. "How old is Molly?" he asked.

Her expression became dreamy and he knew he'd found her key. Whatever part she might play in this sorry scheme, she was a devoted mother. "Molly is three," she admitted. "She's very bright for her age."

"Probably takes after her mother."

Her bleak gesture encompassed the small room. "I hope she'll do better than I've done with my life."

It was too soon, and she was obviously too on edge, for Ben to ask the questions that sprang to his mind. What was her life like that she found it so disappointing? Was it because of Molly? Her own involvement with the kidnappers? What? Instead, Ben asked, "Is this Molly's room?"

"Yes. I'm sorry the bed's so small, but the only alternative was mine."

She had denied being innocent, but her remark so lacked guile that he had trouble believing she was genuine. No one could be that ingenuous in this day and age. "Is that an invitation?" he asked, testing her.

Her face flooded with color. She drew herself up with what looked like real indignation. "It is nothing of the sort, *Your Highness.*"

She gave the title an emphasis that he found puzzling, until he reminded himself that as Prince Nicholas, he was supposed to be happily married and therefore above flirtatious behavior. Too bad Ben Lockhart wasn't half as lucky.

He suppressed a flash of jealousy as he thought of Nicholas's marriage. This was possibly the first time in their lives that Ben had actually envied his royal cousin anything. Ben knew it had a lot to do with Nicholas's happiness that had recently been blessed with the addition of an adorable baby daughter.

Was that why Ben had volunteered to take on this mission, in spite of the danger? He wanted to help end the upheaval in his country, but knew he also wanted to preserve his royal cousin's happiness. As a bachelor himself, Ben had far less to lose than Nicholas.

All their lives, Ben's strong resemblance to his cousin had been more of a curse than a blessing, except perhaps when Ben needed a good table at a busy restaurant. Yet when investigations into the kidnapping of Nicholas's father, King Michael, had reached a stalemate, Ben had offered to exploit his resemblance to Nicholas.

Ben had hoped that the kidnappers would do exactly what they had done, and snatch him in mistake for Nicholas. The rest of the royal family had been against it because of the danger involved, but in the absence of a better plan, Ben had been given the go-ahead.

"Be careful what you wish for," he thought grimly. If flirting wasn't going to help him get information from Meagan, he would have to try another way. Deliberately, he gave a slight groan.

Instantly Meagan's disapproval turned into concern. "What is it?"

He screwed his eyes shut. "Pain in my head. Must be the drug your friends used."

"I'll get something to ease it for you."

He heard the door close behind her and opened his eyes. She returned a moment later and sat down on the side of the bed. "Shane says it's all right to give you these."

"Shane is?"

"My brother." She didn't seem to notice that she had answered his question, as she tipped two white tablets into her palm. She placed the rest of the packet on the dresser and picked up the water glass.

Ben eyed the tablets warily, the memory of being drugged still fresh. "What are they?"

"Painkillers for your headache."

She placed a hand behind his head, helping him raise it so he could swallow the tablets with some of the water. Couldn't hurt, he thought. His muscles ached abominably from the confinement. Once again, the touch of her palm against his neck was a welcome distraction. "Thank you," he said as she eased him back down.

"It's the least I can do."

"You don't like being part of this, do you?"

It was a stab in the dark but it hit home, he saw, as her long lashes came down over those impossibly blue eyes. She glanced back toward the door. "I have no choice."

"You're a prisoner, too?"

"In a way." Her answer was barely audible.

"But isn't this your home?"

She nodded. "That's why Shane brought you here."

"Because no one would suspect you of hiding a kidnapped prince?"

A little of her fire returned to her expression. "It's hardly something I make a habit of doing."

He was relieved to hear it, although he resisted examining his reasons too closely. "Yet you won't help me to escape."

"I can't. It's more than Molly's life is worth."

So her brother and whoever else was party to this scheme were threatening Meagan's daughter. Ben nodded his understanding. "I have a daughter, too," he said, thinking of Nicholas's precious baby girl.

Her gaze softened. "I have an elderly friend who's almost blind. She likes me to read the gossip magazines to her, so I know all about little Princess LeAnn. You must be very proud of her."

He disliked the need to do it, but it was time he gave Meagan a dose of reality. "Right now I'm wondering if I'll ever see her again."

He felt even more of a brute as he saw horror darken her lovely features. He found he wanted to soothe the look away, and actually strained at the ropes in an effort to free his hands. What was he doing? he asked himself as the rope bit into his wrists, a sobering but timely reminder of his situation.

"You'll see her again if I have anything to do with it," she assured him.

"You can't be certain you can protect your own daughter, far less make promises about mine."

"I can try," she said fiercely. "At least Molly is safe enough where she is for now."

"She isn't here?"

"I took her to stay with a friend," she admitted. "The others think she's at a slumber party with some little friends from her play group."

He felt disappointment grip him. "So you were part of this scheme all along."

"No, I…I had a disagreement with my brother yesterday, before I knew they were bringing you here. He threatened Molly, and I decided it was best to get her out of harm's way until I knew more about what Shane had planned. Now I'm glad I did."

"Resourceful of you."

"Comes from fending for myself for most of my life," she said acidly. "Not that you'd know anything about that."

"You'd be surprised," he said dryly. "Royal life has its share of difficulties." His present situation being one of them, he thought.

"I'm sure you've always had a warm bed, and known where your next meal was coming from."

Unlike Meagan? he wondered, reading between the lines. "I can hardly argue," he said. "But speaking of meals…"

She turned pale. "Your food! Shane will wonder what's kept me so long."

"You can always say Prince Nicholas tried to sweet-talk you into letting him go, but you resisted his blandishments," Ben suggested. "It isn't too far from the truth."

"It's also likely to get you beaten."

Ben felt his insides tighten at this idea, but kept his face impassive. "Then you'd have to minister to me some more."

"Or Shane would, and you might not like his ministrations."

"Then work with me. Help me, for the sake of your child and Princess LeAnn."

"No, you don't know what you're asking of me."

She stood up and paced to the window. He watched her graceful movements, feeling his throat go dry. Against all common sense, he was attracted to her, he recognized. If they had met under other circumstances, he would have taken great pleasure in doing something about the attraction.

As it was, he could do nothing. Nor should he. She was the enemy, he made himself remember. No matter how reluctantly she might have become involved, the fact remained that she *was* involved. She had allowed her brother to use her house as a prison for the man she believed to be the country's prince regent. That she had done it under duress didn't lessen her culpability.

It didn't lessen the power of her attractiveness either, Ben thought, feeling warmth flare through him. Her beauty wasn't the whole reason, although he didn't mind feasting his eyes on such loveliness. But he was more attracted to the woman he sensed she was. In their short acquaintance, she had been compassionate and caring toward Ben, willing to risk her brother's displeasure to help Ben as best she was able.

Too bad she thought he was the married Prince Nicholas.

Reluctantly he pulled himself back into the role. "As your future king, I order you to help me."

She turned back, her acid gaze sweeping him. "You're hardly in a position to give orders, Your Highness."

"You would be well rewarded when this is over."

"First flirting with me, now trying to bribe me. What will you try next? Outright seduction?"

He released a heavy sigh. "Why do I get the feeling it wouldn't work anyway?"

"Because it wouldn't." As if from habit she began to tidy the small room, tweaking at the curtains to straighten them, then realigning the items on the dresser.

He watched her in fascination. She wasn't royal but she moved with a quiet, regal grace that was also unconscious. "Are you anti-men or only anti-royalty?"

"Neither," she said, her hands stilling. She held the rag doll as carefully as if it were a baby, he noticed. "For what it's worth, I'm happy living in a monarchy that has kept our country peaceful and prosperous for a thousand years."

"Then that leaves men."

She settled the rag doll on the dresser and turned to him, crossing her arms over her breasts in an angry gesture. "Men are what got me into this mess."

"Surely you mean one man, Molly's father?"

"I mean men, plural. Starting with Molly's father and ending with my brother and his so-called associates and now you."

Ben ached to press her for details about her brother's associates, sensing that they were the key to all this, but he was sure nothing would make her flee faster. "Why include me?" he asked.

"Why not? If it wasn't for you, I wouldn't be in this fix."

"It's hardly my fault," he pointed out, feeling a slow burn of anger start. "I didn't ask to be snatched in the middle of an official engagement, my only crime being who I am."

"Exactly," she said. "You're who you are, and I'm who I am. If it wasn't for this farce, you wouldn't even give me the time of day."

"I'd always give you the time of day, no matter what the situation," he assured her, knowing it was true. She had the sort of face that would stand out in any crowd, and her innate sense of style would have caught his eye, even had she been dressed in rags.

"Really? Next you'll be telling me it doesn't matter that you're the future king of the whole country and I'm a lowly seamstress with a child, barely scraping by."

"Are these your beliefs or your brother's?" he asked on a hunch.

"Mostly my brother's, I suppose," she said bitterly. "I'm not much given to ideology. The only rule I try to live by is the golden rule."

"You can't go far wrong in treating others as you would have them treat you," he agreed. It had been his own philosophy for as long as he could remember. He couldn't resist adding, "Although what you're doing now hardly qualifies."

Her eyes flashed fire at him. "Do you think I don't know that? If there was any other way, believe me I'd take it."

Then he would have to see that he found another way for her, he resolved, not sure exactly how he was supposed to achieve it. Trussed up like a chicken, he wasn't in any position for heroics. "Do you think you could untie me, at least?" he asked.

"Not now," she said with a nervous glance at the closed door.

He took it to mean she might consider it later, if it was safe, and was comforted by the thought. It also meant he would see her again, and he found that notion even more pleasant. He pushed it away in favor of cleansing anger. He had no business thinking of her as anything but his jailer. It was surprisingly hard to do.

Chapter Two

"What do you think you're doing?"

"Making some sandwiches. The prince is hungry."
Meagan braced herself for a blow, but was surprised
to see her brother look repentant. It was a change from
the sneer he usually affected. He was taller than
Meagan and all the low-paying manual jobs he'd done
had made him more muscular, but he stooped slightly
as if he carried the world on his shoulders. She wished
he didn't look so embittered, as if the eight years
between them was more like a hundred.

"Don't flinch away from me as if I'm some kind of
monster. I'm not going to hit you," he said, sounding hurt.

"You did yesterday," she reminded him softly.

"I know, and I'm sorry. I was under pressure,

waiting for word that the kidnapping was on. This isn't an easy time for any of us, but it will be over soon."

She was glad that Shane was behind her, keeping watch through a window, and couldn't see how badly her hands were shaking. Beyond the window, a large shadow moved purposefully back and forth. Shane's friend, Dave, guarding the cottage, she knew. More of the gang members were patrolling between her garden and the edge of the forest. She jerked her head in the direction of Molly's bedroom. "When will this be over? When you kill your prisoner?" Even saying the words made her feel sick to her stomach.

"Nobody's killing anybody, at least not on my watch," he insisted. "Once we get what we need from the prince, we'll let him go."

"Like you did the king?" she couldn't help asking.

Shane pushed his battered Edenbourg Bears cap further back on his head. "Why are you so concerned about these parasites? We're as good as they are. If it wasn't for some ancient laws, and an accident of birth I could be running this country instead of them, rolling in riches and having everybody bow and scrape to me."

"No doubt." She'd heard similar claims from him all their lives. When she was a child she had believed her big brother's grand assertions. She'd wanted to believe them, she knew. Shane had been seventeen when their parents were drowned after a ferry taking them to visit friends on an outer island had capsized in Edenbourg's worst accident at sea. Left behind in

Shane's care, Meagan had been nine. After the tragedy, she had clung to her brother as to a life raft.

He'd promised to take care of her, but had been too young for them to remain together. When she was given into the care of an elderly cousin, Shane had come to see her, assuring her that he would come for her as soon as he was old enough and had made enough money to take care of them both. When Cousin Maude had died, Shane had taken the fifteen-year-old Meagan back to live with him although the promised fortune remained always just over the horizon.

Impressed by his grand-sounding dreams and schemes, she had thought him wonderful. It hadn't taken her long to realize that they would never be more than dreams. He hadn't finished school, telling her it was a waste of his time. When she had asked him why he didn't study at night, he told her he didn't need book learning. The kind of education he needed came from life.

He had supported them with one menial job after another, the latest as a kitchen hand at the castle, using his position to supply his friends with inside information.

She had gradually found out what kind of life really interested Shane. The shady kind where you got what you wanted not from honest effort, but from knowing the wrong people and being prepared to bend the law. It was only good luck that he hadn't spent time in jail yet. He had laughed at her when she decided to use the needlework skill she had inherited from their mother to put herself through school, then gained an apprenticeship to a local dressmaker.

"That kind of progress is too slow for me," he had insisted. "Why don't you join me and my friends? We'll really show you how to have a good time."

She had succumbed just once, long enough to discover that most of Shane's friends were people she wouldn't want to meet in an alley on a dark night. Most of them were Free Edenbourg advocates, a lofty-sounding name for a group of misfits whose main aim was to see the monarchy overthrown.

Never mind that the same monarchy was responsible for a thousand years of peace in the island kingdom located in the North Sea. Meagan got the impression the Frees, as they called themselves, would rather see the country thrown into turmoil, and its assets squandered, than have to bow to another person because of their position.

From what she'd seen of the monarchy, they didn't misuse their inherited power. The opposite in fact. From her studies she knew that much of the progress in the kingdom could be traced to the hard work of the royal family in encouraging tourism and trade and making the country a renowned center of international commerce.

One of Shane's associates, Kevan Slater, a traveling salesman who had shown a brief interest in the group's cause, had seemed different from the others. She allowed herself to think of his name, suppressing the bitterness that welled up when she did. Oh yes, he had seemed different. Until she'd told him she was expecting his child. He'd finally admitted he was married, then disappeared without a trace.

She started when Shane's hand crushed down on her wrist. "That's enough. He has to eat, but you don't have to make it gourmet."

She had barely noticed that her hands had been as busy as her thoughts. Because it was expected of her, she had made a plateful of sandwiches for Shane's friends, then had begun to prepare Nicholas's food. Without conscious design, she had made his more appetizing than the rest. She saw the hungry look Shane gave her handiwork, and made a decision. "This isn't for the prince, it's for you. I'll make another for him."

Her brother gave an approving smile. "You're finally getting your priorities right." He took the sandwich without cutting it in half, and bit into it, smearing mustard across his mouth. "This is good," he said around a mouthful. "Wasted on the likes of his nibs."

Meagan made sure she wasn't too generous this time, while managing to make Nicholas's meal appetizing and nourishing. She had been frightened out of her wits when he was brought here unconscious. She hadn't anticipated that. He had looked terrifyingly pale and she had wondered if he was dead. His slight moan as they dropped him unceremoniously onto Molly's bed had reassured her, even as it alarmed her in case he was injured in some way.

"Wonder what little Molly would think of having a real live royal in her bed," Shane mused, chewing enthusiastically.

"She'd rather have her bedroom and her toys back," Meagan observed.

Shane gestured airily. "She will, soon enough. Provided you keep doing the right thing."

Icy fingers played along Meagan's spine. "You wouldn't really harm her, would you?"

His face darkened. "I shouldn't have said and done what I did yesterday. Trouble is, I'm not sure I can stop the others from harming her if you don't cooperate. You've outsmarted them for now by spiriting her away. But make no mistake, if they want her found they'll find her. Then I won't be answerable for what might happen."

She twisted her hands in despair. "Why have you let them take over your life, Shane? Can't you see, *Frees* is a misnomer if ever there was one. You aren't free. You're a captive of the group's will, even to threatening Molly when I know how much you love her."

Her brother loomed over her, his expression menacing. "Don't say another word. When we get rid of these crowned parasites, and our own people are running things, everything will be different, you'll see. Then I can give you and Molly everything you ever wanted. The Moore name will count for something."

It was the first hint she'd had that his group intended to harm their royal captives. She thought of the people prowling around outside, and shivered. "You mean to kill them, don't you?" she said in a voice barely above a whisper. "Who will run the country then?"

"It's none of your concern."

"But why keep the prince here?" she asked. "Surely it would be better to hold him in a...a more secure location?"

Shane shook his head. "If you think I'm going to blurt out where they've got the king stowed, you're wrong. I'm not that green. Keeping father and son in separate places makes good strategic sense. Your royal friend isn't going anywhere as long as Dave and the team are within earshot. So you may as well accept that you have a houseguest for a while."

He took himself back to the window to finish his sandwich and a bottle of beer he snagged from the table as he went. She looked after him, her heart sinking. It was true that Molly was hidden away with a friend from Meagan's apprenticeship days, Anna Carmody. Meagan had let Anna think she needed some time to finish an urgent dressmaking assignment. But how long would the child remain safe? A group that would kidnap a king and his heir would hardly balk at hurting a three-year-old.

She tidied up the kitchen, gave Shane the food to deliver to the others and picked up another bottle of beer. Her expression defied her brother to comment as she carried the food to the small room where Nicholas lay.

When she walked in he had his eyes closed, giving her a moment to study him. His six-foot frame looked disturbingly large on Molly's diminutive bed. His military-style ceremonial uniform jacket had been thrown over the baby-sized chair so the gold-fringed epaulets brushed the floor, and his white silk shirt and breeches were dust-streaked where the men had dragged him into the car. They still managed to outline his superb physique like a second skin.

The palace would have a gymnasium where he worked out with a personal trainer, she thought, trying to summon the same kind of jealousy she knew Shane harbored. It didn't work. Instead, she had a powerful vision of the prince stripped to the waist hefting some kind of weights, his muscles glistening under the strain. She swallowed hard. She had no business thinking of him in any way at all, far less in a way that made her pulse beat ridiculously fast. The sooner he was out of her house, the sooner she could have Molly home again, safe from any threat, she told herself to dispel the images. Nicholas was merely a means to an end.

He was also married, she reminded herself. From the newspapers, she knew that King Michael's disappearance had happened on the day Nicholas's baby daughter, LeAnn, was to be christened. The entire royal family had gathered for the occasion, but the king's car had crashed on the way to the cathedral. His driver had been drugged and had died in the wreckage. The king's body was never found, and there was speculation that he had been kidnapped, although no ransom demand had been made.

Meagan knew the truth, although she wished she didn't. Shane had boasted that the crash had been set up by his people with help from the group's contact within the royal household. She felt sick even thinking about it. But what could she do? She had risked as much as she dared by telephoning the palace anonymously to let them know the king was still alive. Doing anything more could have dire consequences for her daughter. How could she take the risk?

"I see you've brought my bread and water," Nicholas drawled from the bed. While she was lost in thought he had opened his eyes and caught her studying him. Had he also seen a betrayal of her attraction to him on her face? She hoped not, because she didn't intend to indulge it for one second more. He was married with a child, for goodness sake. He was also the prince regent, acting for the king. What more did she need to convince herself that he was off-limits to her? Surely she wasn't so starved for male company that she could feel drawn to someone so unsuitable?

She set the food down on the dresser. "It may not be the sort of food you're accustomed to at the castle, Your Highness, but it's hardly bread and water."

"It looks fine," he acknowledged with a nod. In the few words they had exchanged, he spoke to her as an equal, she noticed. From the way he acted, he was as gracious as if this was his home and he had invited her to dine with him.

He looked at the bonds restraining his hands. "It's going to be difficult eating or drinking in this position."

"I'm not supposed to untie you," she said, glancing back at the closed door.

"Then you'll have to feed me," he said, sounding as if he found the prospect appealing.

Meagan didn't, but couldn't see that she had much choice. He shimmied over against the wall, but that still left only a sliver of bed for her to perch on, so there was no avoiding contact with him when she sat down. He was as lean and hard as she had expected. What she hadn't expected was the awareness that arced through her, as alarming as it was inappropriate, but she couldn't deny the strength of it.

"Your hands are trembling," he said as she pulled off a corner of sandwich and placed it between his lips. His teeth grazed her fingers, notching her sense of awareness up several degrees in intensity.

"Stop talking and eat," she said, as annoyed with herself as with him for making her feel things she had no business feeling.

He ate. "This is good," he said after several bites. "I might wash it down with some of that beer now."

"This isn't room service," she snapped, driven almost to fever pitch by the enforced closeness. She could swear he was needlessly skimming his mouth over her fingers, heightening the contact, as if well aware of the effect he was having on her.

His wide shoulders lifted. "Then untie me and I'll drink the beer myself. I'm a big boy."

Of that she had no doubt. "Nice try, Your Highness," she said, lifting the foaming bottle to his mouth.

He drank eagerly, as if thirst was a bigger problem than hunger. When she pulled the bottle away, foam rimmed his upper lip. Without thinking, she used a clean handkerchief to wipe it away. The gesture was so intimate that her breath hitched. He felt it too, she saw from the way his eyes darkened and he dragged in air.

"Why are you doing this?" he asked in a husky tone. "Even if they are threatening your child, there are people you can turn to for help."

"You don't know these people the way I do."

"Is Molly's father still part of the conspiracy?" It would explain her reluctance to turn them in, Ben thought.

"He's…" In time she stopped herself from revealing too much. Shane was right, Nicholas was clever, but she couldn't let herself be manipulated by him. Her daughter's life could depend on it. "I've already told you too much."

"You haven't told me one thing that's useful," he said on a note of frustration. "If you really don't want to be involved, you could help me get a message back to the castle."

Part of her longed to do as he asked. Was it because she was really a lackey of royalty as Shane suggested, or because there was something warm and compassionate in Nicholas's eyes that she responded to instinctively? Either way, she couldn't risk Molly's safety, not even for him. "I can't," she denied. "The last time I tried to do something, I paid for it dearly."

She saw his gaze reflect sudden comprehension. "You were the one who called the palace anonymously, with the news that the king is still alive, weren't you?"

She shook her head. "Whoever it was, it wasn't me."

He didn't believe her, she saw from his skeptical look. "But he is still alive?"

"Yes, but he's ill, so they needed you, although I'm not sure why. I don't know where he's being held. Not here," she added quickly. "They didn't want the two of you in the same place."

"Too easy to stage a rescue," he concluded. "It's what I'd do if the tables were turned."

She couldn't imagine him holding anyone against their will, and wondered how she could be so sure. She only knew she was. "If you've had enough to eat and drink, I have to go," she said, suddenly anxious to put as much distance between them as she could.

He shifted in apparent discomfort, an expression of pain invading his face. "Could you at least untie me for a few minutes? My shoulders are killing me."

"In a while. My brother will be going out to a meeting," she said.

"Then I'll have to try to be patient," he said. "Just don't stay away too long. I might get hungry again."

His tone suggested that he didn't mean for food, and she felt her face heat. Telling herself that he was only trying to gain her confidence didn't help. "Next time, one of the men can come and feed you."

"Pity. I was starting to enjoy that perfume you wear."

"I bought it to celebrate getting the commission to design the dresses for an entire wedding party, not to please you," she stated, sounding put out.

His eyes lit with interest. "You're a designer?"

"A dressmaker. Nothing as fancy as a designer."

"You made the furnishings in this room?"

She felt her color deepen, although she hated him to think she cared whether or not he noticed. "Yes, although they're probably nothing compared to what you're used to."

"I live a lot more modestly than you think," he said.

"But I'd wager that you're as good with a needle as any court decorator I've ever seen."

"I sincerely doubt it, but thank you for the compliment, Your Highness."

"It's not a compliment, it's a statement of fact," he growled. "A compliment is when I tell you that your hair reminds me of spun sunshine, and that your eyes are the color of lapis lazuli."

If he had expected to please her, he was mistaken. "That's no way for a married man to talk," she snapped. "You're making me wonder if the magazines portray you accurately."

"How do they portray me?" he asked, curious in spite of himself.

"You must have read some of the stories."

He shook his head. "I read as little about myself as I can."

"Then it isn't up to me to feed your ego," she snapped. "As the heir and now the prince regent, I'm sure you get more compliments than are good for one person."

Ben looked annoyed. "Obviously you intend to be the exception."

"I'm sorry if it's not what you're accustomed to. I wasn't brought up with courtly manners. I'd be more at home with that cousin of yours, the one who's supposed to resemble you."

"Ben Lockhart," the prince supplied.

"That's right. From what I've read, he has the best of both worlds, a royal background, and the freedom to live his life his way."

"So you think Ben would be more attractive than me?"

"At least he isn't married." Snatching up the plate and empty beer bottle, she almost ran from the room, wondering why she felt an overpowering need to escape. Nicholas was the prisoner here, not she. Yet with his charming manner and honeyed words, she felt as if he had somehow captured a part of her soul.

Shane's associates weren't the only threat to her, she realized with a frisson of alarm. In his way, the acting king was an even greater danger to her peace of mind. As long as Nicholas remained under her roof, she would have to be on her guard against him.

Once before, she had allowed a man to sweet-talk his way into her life with promises of forever. Molly had been the result. Meagan knew she wouldn't trade her daughter for all the riches in the kingdom, but she wasn't about to fall under any man's spell again, especially one who was married with a baby daughter. With him, forever would be even briefer than it had been with Molly's father.

It didn't stop Nicholas's words from haunting her as she went about her chores. Or prevent her spirits from taking an upward leap when Shane jammed his cap onto his head and announced that he was going out. Dave was on call if she needed him, her brother told her. He didn't add that the people patrolling the forest would stop her doing anything foolish like trying to help Nicholas escape, although she got the message. But for now, she and Nicholas were alone in the house.

Chapter Three

By now Ben had worked out the best way to free himself if he wanted to, although he had to give full credit to whoever had tied him up. It was a professional job, but no match for a navy lieutenant. In the service he'd won many a bet untying knots, although not usually when they were around his wrists. Even so, these should be a breeze, he thought, hoping he wasn't being overly optimistic.

Satisfied, he left the ropes alone, although the growing numbness in his arms tempted him to do otherwise. He was likely to learn more by continuing to work at winning Meagan's confidence then getting *her* to untie him. She had said she didn't know where the king was being held, but she might know more than she realized.

Thinking of Meagan, he frowned. She had admitted she was being forced into helping the conspirators to protect her three-year-old child. By using her, would Ben put the child in jeopardy himself? He didn't like the thought, any more than he liked taking advantage of the obvious attraction he had felt vibrating between him and Meagan at first sight.

It was pure chemistry, he told himself. He felt sorry for her situation, but he wasn't going to let any woman capture his heart ever again, no matter how attractive she was. He couldn't deny that he was attracted to her, but he also couldn't deny that she came from a family that liked living on the edge. She had admitted that her brother was up to his neck in this conspiracy.

Meagan reminded him too much of Marina, Ben thought, expecting to feel the familiar gut-wrenching sorrow. To his amazement, all that came was a dull sadness, as if the anguish of his fiancée's death was finally starting to dim. Maybe he should expect it by now. Or maybe a golden-haired Cinderella had distracted him sufficiently to drown out the painful memories.

He braced himself as the door opened, relaxing when he saw that it was Meagan. She carried a carafe of water. Again he was intrigued by her graceful movements, as if she were acting to music only she could hear.

"My brother's gone to his meeting, Your Highness," she said.

He watched her pour water into the glass on the dresser. "So we're alone now?"

Some of the water spilled onto the dresser. Good. He wasn't the only one feeling the air vibrate between them.

She took a child's towel out of a drawer and mopped up the spill, then turned to him, clutching the towel like a security blanket. "There's no one else in the house, but Shane has people patrolling the garden and the woods."

"So there's no reason not to untie me."

"How do I know you won't try to escape?"

"Isn't the word of your crown prince good enough for you?"

She didn't seem to notice that he hadn't exactly given it. "I suppose so. But you must let me tie you up again before Shane returns. And stay away from the window. I dare not let the others find out I've released you."

He fixed her with a dazzling smile. "I wouldn't want to get you in trouble with your friends."

"They're not my friends." She put the towel down and perched on the edge of the bed, leaning across him as she started to work on the ropes. He could have undone them in half the time, but it was undeniably more pleasant lying there with her delicate body pressed against him, basking in her delicious rose scent. "You're not at all what I expected royalty to be like," she observed.

His breathing had shallowed, and he felt his heart gather speed as he asked, "What did you expect?"

"Arrogance, perhaps. Less consideration for your subjects."

He wouldn't have a lot of consideration for this subject if she didn't hurry up, he thought. If she truly didn't know what her closeness was doing to him, she must be more innocent than she gave herself credit for. "The royal family's position is one of service to the people of Edenbourg. It doesn't leave much room for arrogance."

She caught her full lower lip between ivory teeth. "That's not what Shane says. According to his group the royal family are parasites, sucking the people dry."

Finally freed, Ben pulled his hands down, grimacing as the blood flowed painfully into his arms and hands. He flexed them, wishing he could exercise them more gainfully, say by putting them around her. "What do you think?"

She lowered long lashes over her eyes, as if afraid of revealing too much. "I don't agree with them."

He found the admission more pleasing than he had any business doing, and made himself remember his objective. "Tell me more about these friends of your brother's."

She stood up, shaking her head. "It's more than Molly's life is worth."

He swung his legs over the edge of the bed and took her hands, fascinated to see how small they were in his large ones. He felt the calluses on her fingers and suppressed a frown. She had said her life was hard, so her hands would be workworn. He was surprised at how little he liked the thought. "You said your child is safe for now. I can make sure she stays that way."

Her huge eyes flooded and she blinked hard. "If you only could…"

"Trust me."

"Your Highness, I'd like to, but…"

He guessed the rest. "Someone else taught you the folly of trusting too much. Who was he, Meagan?"

She shot him a startled look, reminding him of a fawn he'd photographed once in the royal forest. "How do you know it was a man?"

He released a sigh. "It invariably is."

He decided not to press his luck too hard right away. When he uncoiled from the tiny bed, he was careful not to move too fast, frightening her into calling for help. He had seen a large shadow pass the window at regular intervals.

He dropped to the floor and drove himself into a quick set of push-ups to get his blood circulating again, irritated to find he enjoyed the gasp of admiration they elicited from Meagan.

When he finally stood up, he felt much better. She looked thunderstruck. "Haven't you seen a man do push-ups before?"

"Not like those."

"Doesn't your brother work out?" he asked.

"I wouldn't know. He doesn't live here."

Another piece of useful information to be filed for later use. "Is there anywhere I can get some air?" he asked. A glimpse of the outside might give him a clue to his whereabouts.

She tilted her head to one side, thinking. "No one will see you in the courtyard. This way."

She opened the second door, not into a closet as he'd

thought, but into a stone-walled outdoor area about
three meters long in each direction. Violets grew
between silvered cobblestones underfoot, and ivy
softened the high stone walls. In the center stood a
wrought-iron love seat also entwined with ivy. "This
is Molly's secret garden," Meagan said. "It's the reason
I fell in love with this house."

"A child's imagination would work overtime in a
place like this," he agreed, stepping into the courtyard.
The fresh air filled his lungs, invigorating him. The sun's
position told him it was late afternoon, so he'd been
here for about six hours. Conscious for three, therefore
out cold for three. He remembered being bundled into
a car before the drug claimed him completely, giving
him a radius of a hundred or so kilometers from his
starting point that morning. Not much help.

"You're on the outskirts of Old Stanbury, near the
forest," she second-guessed him. "The house is fairly
isolated so there's no point calling for help."

He had already worked that out for himself. There
was no gate but he had sized up the stone wall as being
easier to climb than the pitching ratlines of a ship in a
storm-tossed sea, which he'd done many times while
indulging in his hobby of sailing old vessels.

He wondered if Meagan's unseen brother and his
friends knew what an unsuitable prison his sister's
house made. Luckily for them, escape wasn't on Ben's
agenda just yet. Not until he'd learned a lot more.

He dropped his hands to her slender shoulders. "I
know you want to help me, Meagan. Why stop at

hints? Why not follow your heart and help rescue your prince?"

Meagan felt the heat of his hands like a brand through her thin dress, yet his touch was light, leaving her free to move away if she wanted to. She didn't. His hands on her shoulders reminded her of how long it had been since any man had touched her, making her ache for more.

He was her ruler, she reminded herself. But she found herself responding to him more as a man, and a very attractive man at that.

She did twist free then, shocked at her thoughts. Nicholas was married with a child. That he was willing to use his masculinity to try to manipulate her made him no better than Molly's father.

"I want to help you, Your Highness, but you mustn't touch me," she said, knowing she sounded stupidly prim, but unable to help it.

"I won't unless you want me to," he promised, his voice low and reassuring.

"How can I want you to? You're acting for the king and you're a married man."

A shadow tinged his eyes, making her wonder if he felt as drawn to her as she did to him, in spite of the inappropriateness of it. "You're right," he said heavily. He passed a hand across the lower half of his face. "I've heard about the bond that forms between kidnapper and captive, but I didn't think it happened so quickly."

"I'm sure it doesn't." She was aware of sounding as if she wanted to believe it. "You'd better come back inside before Shane returns."

He hadn't learned anything useful, Ben thought in frustration. He knew roughly where he was, but not where his uncle, King Michael, was being held. Ben didn't like it, but he would have to take advantage of the attraction between him and Meagan to try to learn more. That he might want to for his own sake, he resisted examining. He turned as if to walk back inside, steering her until she was between himself and the iron bench.

Meagan recognized that she was trapped. She felt her heartbeat gather speed as the prince left no more than a handspan of space between them. Oddly enough she wasn't afraid, although she probably should have been. Nicholas was large enough and fit enough to overpower her if he chose to. But the nerves scrambling inside her felt less like fear, and more like the response of a woman to an attractive man.

Reminding herself that he was, first and foremost, her ruler, failed to subdue the tremors gripping her. Neither did telling herself that her feelings were only a product of having him captive in her house. Under normal circumstances, he wouldn't even acknowledge her existence, far less look at her in the desirous way he was doing now, she felt sure.

Had she been a fool to release him, accepting his word that he wouldn't try anything untoward? She should know better than to trust any man's word by now. Yet reminding herself of her earlier foolishness with Molly's father didn't stop Meagan's lips from drying as she imagined the prince's mobile mouth on hers. Picturing herself in his arms was easier still, and her own arms ached with the need to be held, to be caressed, to be loved.

By him?

What was it about Prince Nicholas that put such thoughts in her head? Meagan tried to cool the heat surging through her. Kevan had also been married, she had discovered when she'd told him she was expecting his child. When he had turned her away, she had vowed never again to allow a man to use her so cruelly. Yet here she was, gripped by a desire so strong that she could hardly breathe.

Her imagination insisted on picturing herself alone with Nicholas, not under duress with guards a shout away, but truly alone. Butterflies danced in her stomach. She felt frightened now, but not of him. Of herself and what he made her feel.

Ben had seen the flames ignite in her eyes, and was convinced that she felt as tormented as he did by the firestorm of attraction raging between them. He wished he could trust her enough to reveal his real identity. Then there would be nothing to stop him from taking her in his arms and drinking his fill of her sweetness.

He imagined shaping her mouth to his and parting her lips gently to taste the honey within, and a fist of longing slammed through him.

Her sigh sounded loud in the quiet space, firing him with needs and desires he had barely acknowledged since Marina died. Instead, he had plunged into work, gaining a reputation as a hotshot who could pilot anything. That was a laugh. Right now it was all he could do to pilot himself through the treacherous shoals of one woman's attraction.

Meagan wanted him as much as he wanted her, he realized in some astonishment. She looked as if she had completely forgotten that she was his jailer. And she made him want to forget.

He restrained himself from taking her into his arms and instead, pulled her down with him onto the bench, keeping a careful heartbeat of distance between them. He wished he could tell her it was all right, he wasn't who she thought he was. He was free to give her everything in his power, taking only what she was willing to give in return. He sensed it would be a great deal.

What was he thinking about? The very reason he was free to give her so much argued against giving her anything at all. She was on the other side, no matter how reluctantly. He had a job to do and this was hardly the way to do it. The reminder had little effect on the flames leaping inside him. Knowing he couldn't have her only made him want her more.

He told himself he could learn more by deception than by outright confrontation, but knew he wasn't being honest with himself. He didn't want to kiss Meagan out of duty, but purely for his own satisfaction, and the pleasure he knew they could give each other.

She angled her body slightly away from him, signaling her rejection of what they both knew had nearly happened between them. "You're royalty and you have a family waiting for you." She sounded as regretful as he felt.

Honor and duty could be a curse, he thought on an inward sigh, intrigued by the dusting of rose his closeness had placed on her cheeks, and the bedroom look he had stirred in her eyes. Why couldn't they have met under different circumstances, when he wouldn't have had to work so hard to resist that look? After Marina, he had thought he would never feel this way again. Too bad it had to happen with the last woman in Edenbourg who should interest him.

"We must go in," she prompted. "I have to tie you up again before Shane finds out I let you go."

Ben caught her shoulders and made her look at him. "You don't have to do this, Meagan. You can help me. Think of your little girl."

He recoiled from the bleakness that invaded her gaze, recognizing that the moment of closeness was over. He should have taken advantage of it while he had the chance, he told himself, but couldn't make himself regret his inaction. He would find some other way to complete his mission, without using a woman who deserved better.

"I am thinking of her. Will you come in, or do I have to call for help?"

He went in.

"Can I at least use your bathroom first?" he asked when she gestured toward the bed.

She took him through the first door into a passageway. The whitewashed walls and polished wooden floor gave him no more clues, and she barred his way when he would have explored further. "The bathroom's in there."

He could have forced his way past her, but wasn't ready for that yet. He didn't want to put her or her child at further risk unless he had to. "Sure you don't want to come in and bathe me?"

He was pleased to see that her association with her brother's friends hadn't hardened her so much that she couldn't still blush. "You're big enough to manage on your own." Her color heightened further as it dawned on her there were different ways he could take this.

He decided not to push it, but couldn't resist asking, "How do you know I won't slip through the window?"

"You won't."

He soon saw why. The mullioned window was far too small to accommodate his wide shoulders. He did what he needed to, then skimmed a quick look through her bathroom cabinet. Beyond an assortment of toiletries and baby-care items, he found no new clues to his beautiful jailer. But he did find the source of the wonderful rose scent—a small laboratory of essential oils and floral fragrances.

He picked up a bottle with a hand-written label, removed the glass stopper and inhaled deeply. Definitely Meagan's scent. It would be a long time before he could smell roses again without thinking of her.

She was waiting when he returned to the hall. On the wall behind her was a framed photograph of Meagan and a toddler who looked so like a miniature version of her mother that she had to be Molly. "Your daughter looks a lot like you," he commented.

"People say she takes after me."

"Not her father?"

Meagan shook her head, her expression shuttered as she opened the door into the bedroom again.

Lying down and letting her tie his hands again took a lot of self-discipline. She didn't do as professional a job as whoever had done it the first time, he noted, worried that her amateur effort might be harder to undo than the more skilled version which at least had followed a predictable pattern.

There was nothing he could do about it now except try to stop himself from responding to the feel of her moving against him as she tested the ropes. "Do they look all right to you?" she asked.

Considering that when she leaned across him, stretching out her arms to adjust his bonds, her full breasts were aligned with his mouth, he could only give a strangled affirmative. He knew she wasn't as innocent as she looked, yet she seemed unaware of the effect she had on him every time she brushed so intimately against him.

"Comfortable?" she asked.

He almost choked. He was glad she had thrown a light coverlet over him so she couldn't see that he was far from comfortable. He didn't know if it was being bound like this, helpless in her hands, but he had never felt so aroused in his life. The remembered closeness between them in the courtyard vibrated through him, making him strain automatically to free his arms so he could bring them around her. Just as well he couldn't. He didn't think he could keep up the white knight act and maintain his distance in the face of such temptation.

"They'll do," she pronounced, standing up. "I have to go. Shane will be back soon."

"Will you come and feed me again?" Ben asked hopefully.

She shook her head. "One of the others will do it. I have to go out."

"To see Molly?"

"Yesterday I took her away in such a hurry that I forgot her favourite teddy bear, Mr. Snug. She won't sleep without him."

Ben cocked his head at the threadbare toy sitting on the pillow near his head. "Mr. Snug, I presume."

She nodded and tucked the bear into the crook of her arm. "If Shane misses me, I'll tell him I had to go to the store for groceries."

"How can you be certain you won't be followed?"

"I took the precaution of flushing some milk and other foodstuffs down the sink, so it looks as if we've run out of a few things. It's the only plan I can think of that has a chance of working. But I can't stand the thought of Molly crying herself to sleep tonight. This is the longest she's been away from me."

Harder for Meagan herself, he suspected. He was tempted to ask her to send a message to the castle for him, but knew she'd be lucky to get away without being stopped as it was. Another thought occurred to him. "Why didn't you go now, instead of coming to me?"

"I…I didn't want the others to see which way I was really going."

She had also wanted to help him, Ben read into her hesitation, unwillingly gratified by the thought, although he told himself she believed she was helping the crown prince. "Thank you for sticking around anyway," he said gruffly.

Her expression confirmed his suspicion, but he saw her mask it quickly. "I was only thinking of Molly," she said.

He hadn't been thinking of her daughter when he wanted to kiss the mother, Ben thought when he was alone again. He hadn't been thinking of anything except how pleasurable it would be to hold Meagan in his arms. He ached to have it become a reality.

Except that it wasn't going to happen. When this was over, she could well go to jail for her part in the king's abduction. Ben would testify to her kindness toward him, but would it be enough? He had only her word that she was in this against her will.

He dismissed the doubt as quickly as it arose. The fear he had seen in her eyes was genuine, he would swear to it. She was as much a victim as the king was. Ben hoped it would convince a judge not to send her to prison, but he wouldn't like to count on it. What would become of little Molly then?

Ben forced his mind away from that question. He had more pressing worries, like how to free himself. Meagan's ham-fisted attempt at knot-tying was proving as great a challenge as he'd feared. As he worked away at the rope, trying to loosen his bonds while ignoring the growing pain in his wrists where the rope bit into him, he reviewed the few details he had gleaned so far.

He was in a modest cottage on the edge of the forest near the old part of the city. The king was still alive but in poor health and being held in another part of the city. The group Meagan's brother belonged to was behind the whole thing, but Ben was becoming convinced that they were acting under orders from someone at the palace.

Ben didn't like to think of a member of the royal family being involved, but it had to be faced. Who? Jake Stanbury had been exonerated. There was King Michael's brother, Edward, and his son, Luke, back in Edenbourg after years of estrangement. Ben could see how much Edward loved Michael, despite their long separation. And his eldest son Luke had worked hard to bring about a reconciliation between the brothers. So who did that leave? Ben knew he wasn't likely to solve the riddle tonight.

He was brought a mug of soup by a hulking brute of a man he guessed was the guard whose shadow he had seen passing the window at regular intervals. Of Shane himself, Ben had seen nothing but he guessed he would soon, and wasn't looking forward to it. Any man who would threaten his own sister and niece was unlikely to be pleasant company.

"Do you have a name?" he asked the guard without much hope of a helpful answer.

To Ben's surprise, the man stammered, "D-d-dave."

"What's your involvement in this business, Dave?"

The man merely snarled and lifted Ben's head so he could drink the soup. It wasn't nearly as much fun as when Meagan did the same thing, Ben thought, gagging as some of the soup went down too fast. He made himself swallow as much as he could, knowing he needed to keep his strength up. But he managed to learn nothing more from the inarticulate giant who swabbed his mouth with a none-too-clean cloth. That would have been the end of their interaction, but Ben protested that he'd better be escorted to the bathroom. Grunting, Dave complied, then tied Ben up again and left him alone.

He tried to sleep without much success. Too uncomfortable. But thinking of Meagan made him even more uncomfortable. He was afraid it was going to be a long night.

Chapter Four

Meagan wondered if she looked as terrible as she felt. Last night she had barely slept at all. Seeing Molly had lifted her spirits immeasurably, but had made returning to the house alone so much harder to bear.

Bad though her night had been, the prince's must have been much less pleasant, Meagan thought. This morning she had almost stopped by Molly's room to assure herself that Nicholas was all right, but had resisted. She'd told herself she hadn't wanted to anger her brother, but suspected she wasn't prepared to deal with Nicholas's effect on her.

Last night, as she'd tossed and turned, he had haunted her thoughts, and when she had dropped into moments of fitful sleep, he had been in her dreams. He was her prince regent and he was in dire trouble, so she should be concerned, she told herself. But nowhere in that concern should she feel the desire that accompanied thoughts of him.

She felt it now, shaming her, as she tried to concentrate on embroidering a new dress for Molly's birthday in a month's time. Yesterday Meagan hadn't given in to the temptation to kiss him, but she had wanted to more than she had wanted anything in a long time.

Her fingers faltered on the tiny, precise stitches. She worked to no pattern save the one in her mind, usually so nimble and sure of her task that she barely thought about it. Today she sewed like the rawest apprentice, fumbling the simplest stitches. One name served as explanation. *Nicholas.*

Nicholas? Over the ticking of the carriage clock on the mantelpiece, she shaped his name between dry lips, wondering why it sounded wrong somehow. She couldn't make it fit the man in Molly's room, although she had seen him pictured with his family countless times in the magazines she read aloud to her elderly friend.

Muttering to herself, she began to unpick an imperfect stitch. Next she would be denying that he was married and would eventually be her king. How much simpler this would have been if he had been the prince's cousin, the dashing bachelor, Ben Lockhart.

This time, the name rolled easily off her tongue and she savored the sound of it, before she became angry with herself. How often had she told Molly that wishing didn't make something so? The royal cousins might look alike, but Shane wouldn't have risked everything to capture a navy lieutenant.

But what if...she drove the thought away. How hard was she prepared to work at justifying wanting a man she couldn't, shouldn't want?

Shane would be furious if he knew how much time she had spent with the prince yesterday before sneaking away to see Molly. Meagan had managed to return only minutes before Shane came back from his meeting. She was glad she hadn't needed her cover story about shopping for groceries because she was sure her heightened color would have betrayed her.

When Shane returned, she had been shocked to see how pale and drawn he looked. Perhaps he wasn't as comfortable as he pretended to be with what his friends had dragged him into.

He didn't look any happier now as he joined her in the living room. "Shall I get you some coffee?" she asked.

"No thanks." He moved up beside her chair and she caught her breath. She knew it wasn't only because she feared being found out. Shane had changed lately. He had always been moody, but these days he had a hair-trigger temper as well.

He had shown it when he caught her telephoning the castle anonymously to tell them the king was still alive. She had made the call from a telephone booth well away from the house, but he had spotted her as he drove past. He had listened in on the call long enough to learn the truth, before slamming the receiver down, cutting her off in mid-sentence.

Afterward he had ranted at her like a madman, accusing her of betraying him and threatening to make her regret her actions if she crossed him again. She had burst into tears, shocking him, but the damage was done.

He had controlled his temper around her until she had asked him not to use her cottage as a meeting place for his fellow conspirators. He had struck her across the face. As with the first occurrence, he had repented immediately, begging her to forgive him, but she knew she wouldn't relax around him for a long time to come.

Now, as she turned and saw accusation on his face, she braced herself.

Her apprehension was justified when he said, "Did you enjoy your visit with Molly yesterday?"

Horror sliced through her, but she kept her expression bland as she tucked the needle into the fabric and folded her hands over it. "I did go out, but only to the store to get groceries. If you don't believe me, look in the kitchen cupboards."

Shane's mouth angled into a sneer. "Nice try. But when I checked on our prisoner this morning, Molly's teddy bear wasn't on the pillow, although it was there when we brought his nibs here. So I checked the mileage on your car. Either you took the long way to the store, or you went somewhere further afield. My guess is you visited either your old schoolteacher, Violet, or your friend Anna. You wouldn't leave Molly with a doddery old spinster with failing eyesight, so that leaves Anna Carmody."

Meagan placed her sewing into the basket at her feet, averting her face to hide her alarm. "I told you Molly was staying at her friend's place. After you brought Prince Nicholas here, I called the girl's mother and asked if Molly could stay another night. Don't worry, I said I was ill. But I did go to see Violet. She isn't well, so I took her some essential oils from my collection. Then I sat and read to her for a while."

"The story of Raggedy-May and Strawbie," he said with a sneer, referring to the favorite Edenbourg children's fairy-tale characters. Molly loved the stories so much that Meagan had made her a Raggedy-May doll of her own. The little girl had cried for the doll last night, Meagan remembered with a pang. She had been so overwrought she hadn't thought to take the doll as well as the teddy bear.

Shane was telling her he wasn't fooled, she thought, trembling inwardly. She struggled to hide her panic. "I read from the *Edenbourg Ladies' Journal*," she insisted. "Violet loves me to read her the latest gossip."

Shane gave a dismissive shrug. "Have it your way. Don't worry, I won't tell the others where you've stashed Molly unless you force me to. Blood is thicker than water, after all."

She heard the implied threat and shuddered. She was Shane's flesh and blood, too, but he seemed to have forgotten that part. What had happened to them? As children they had been so close, even when she had been sent to live with Cousin Maude after their parents died. Lonely and constrained by the strict old lady's regimen,

Meagan had lived for Shane's weekly visits and had been overjoyed when they could be a family again.

Now everything was different. Meagan believed that the monarchy was the country's future, and Shane couldn't wait to see them gone. Suddenly she recalled a game they had played when they were children, when their dear parents had still been alive and they were a real family.

They had played a favorite Edenbourg children's game called Kings and Subjects. Molly played it now with her dolls, Meagan thought fondly. Naturally, Shane had insisted on being the king with Meagan as his subject.

He had acted the way he thought kings acted, pushing her around and issuing peremptory rulings that made very little sense. "Go and stand over there," he would say. When she did, he would immediately order her to stand somewhere else. When she asked why he acted so illogically, he said that was how royals behaved. When she argued, he decreed that subjects had no right to talk back to the king.

It wasn't how Nicholas behaved, she thought. He hadn't tried to give her orders. He had spoken to her like a normal person.

He had come within a heartbeat of kissing her.

Shane would kill her if he knew how tempted she'd been to let it happen, or how little she regretted the moment of closeness. Nicholas's attention made her feel vibrantly alive. Shane would say it was because the prince was a master of seduction. Before he married he had been known as the playboy prince, although he was supposed to have become an exemplary husband. Not so exemplary if he could have such an effect on her, she thought.

What was she thinking? Meagan's hand flew to her mouth as she realized how condemnatory her thoughts were. Nicholas *was* married, and to a woman the people of Edenbourg had taken to their hearts. How could Meagan justify wanting him to kiss her when he had no right to look at any other woman?

It didn't stop her from imagining the feel of his mouth on hers, or wishing that he wasn't married. She wasn't sure what kind of woman that made her. Perhaps she was as amoral as Shane had accused her of being when he'd found out that she was pregnant with Molly.

She hadn't been able to see that Kevan was only using her, and had believed him when he'd told her he loved her. Although, as a traveling salesman, his visits had been unpredictable, depending on his business activities. He had come to her apparently in anguish one night, telling her that his mother had died and he had no one to turn to but her. She had never suspected it was a ruse.

Shane always said Meagan's heart was too soft for her own good. That night it had been true. She had allowed Kevan to stay and pour out his heart to her. When he came into her arms and rested his head against her, she hadn't suspected that it was only the first step in a practised seduction designed to lead her into bed before the night was over.

Molly had been the result. After sustaining Kevan when he needed her, she had expected support from him when she told him her news. After all, he'd promised he'd taken precautions against her getting pregnant. And it was her first time, so she trusted him. Then he had told her the awful news, that he was married with two children. For his children's sake Meagan hadn't pursued him, but had determined never to be so gullible again.

Yet here she was, mooning over another married man. She *knew* that Nicholas was married, so what was her excuse this time? She had none, she acknowledged to herself.

"I hope you're not scheming to help our royal visitor," Shane said as if reading her thoughts. "I'd hate to see any harm come to Molly because you insisted on acting foolishly."

The threat made a fist-sized lump swell in her throat. "How could I possibly help him, when you have him guarded day and night?"

"You might take it into your head to call the castle again."

She reached into her work basket for a skein of colored thread and began to wind it onto a wooden bobbin so Shane wouldn't see how badly her hands were shaking. "I told you, the last call was a mistake."

Shane grasped the back of her neck and gave her a slight shake. "Just as long as you don't make any more."

Her skin crawled. "How long do you plan to keep the prince here?"

"I'm surprised you object, since you apparently find him attractive."

"I don't…" she began, then her voice tailed off as Dave hustled Prince Nicholas into the living room, his arms bound behind his back. His silk shirt and breeches had been replaced with a pair of khaki homespun pants and a traditional Edenbourg peasant's shirt with full sleeves, the front slashed almost to the waist.

Nicholas's eyebrow lifted as his gaze fell on her. "Still on the side of the devil, Meagan?"

As Dave pushed Nicholas roughly into a chair alongside hers, she drew a sharp breath. What she had taken to be the shadow of beard along his jawline, she now saw was a bruise, as if he had been struck a vicious blow across the face. Compassion flooded through her and she wished there was some way she could help him.

Even now, injured and bound, he maintained a defiant air. Dave towered over him as he did most men, yet Nicholas had obviously put up a fight anyway. "Are you all right?" she asked, knowing she risked Shane's censure, but needing to know anyway.

Nicholas flexed his jaw as if testing it. "Everything still works, but Dave here won't be courting the ladies for a few days."

Dave grunted and lashed out, catching Nicholas across the back of the head. Meagan gave a cry of objection and jumped up, but Shane came between her and the giant. "Cool it, both of you. We only want to have a talk with the prince."

Nicholas eased his head from side to side, wincing as if in pain. "You must be Shane. Talk away. It will save me the trouble."

Dave lifted his arm again but Shane caught his hand in midair. "Enough. He can't talk if you break his jaw. You might have to later, but first let's give him the chance to cooperate."

Meagan felt relieved when the giant went outside, grunting to himself. She started to leave, unable to bear the sight of Nicholas being tormented when there was nothing she could do to prevent it. But Shane motioned her back to the chair. "Stay, you might learn something."

She sat, gripping the arm rests until her knuckles whitened. "Such as how to beat a man whose hands are tied?"

Nicholas shot her a regal glare. "Stay out of this, Meagan, it isn't your fight."

She was amazed that the prince would put her safety ahead of his own even now. Couldn't he see that he could get himself hurt or killed? Fear for him warred with pride that he considered her worth the risk.

Shane moved to stand over the prince's chair. "Oh, but it is her fight. As long as the country is divided into royalty and the rest, it's everybody's fight."

Nicholas shook his head. "Your people are the only ones dividing the country. Give this up now. Return King Michael and me to the castle safely, and you'll be treated fairly. You have my word on it."

She closed her eyes in a fleeting prayer, then opened them again. "Shane, listen to him. It isn't too late."

Shane spun to look at her. "What did he offer you to side with him? Money? A position at the castle? Maybe the chance to serve as his mistress? That's it, isn't it? He wasn't known as the playboy prince for nothing. Leopards don't change their spots that easily."

With the force of a whipcrack, Nicholas's voice cut through Shane's tirade. "I offered her nothing of the sort, and even if I'd tried—which I didn't—she's too much of a lady to value herself so cheaply. If my hands weren't tied, I'd flatten you for making such a vile suggestion."

Shane planted both hands on the arms of the prince's chair. "It's easy to be a big man when you know you don't have to back up your threats."

Nicholas matched him glare for glare. "Untie me and I'll gladly back them up."

Her heartbeat raging, Meagan stood and pushed Shane away from Nicholas. "You said you wanted to talk, not argue over me. My opinions are my own, and I resent the suggestion that I can be bought by anyone. I won't be used as a pawn—by either of you," she added, glaring at Prince Nicholas.

He looked…he looked amused, she thought in amazement. How could he possibly find anything amusing about this situation? Didn't he understand that in his present frame of mind, Shane was capable of violence? Yet she couldn't deny the spark she saw in the prince's dark gaze, as if he found her defense of him as engaging as it was unnecessary.

Again, it came to her that he seemed more sure of

himself than was warranted, as if this was all part of some plan. But it couldn't be, unless…

…Unless her suspicions were correct and he was part of some trap set for Shane and his group. A trap that would ensnare her as well. She couldn't care about that now. She wanted this to be over. Kidnapping wasn't right, any more than were her feelings for Nicholas.

A pang gripped her. Surely her first loyalty should be to Shane? Should she share her suspicion with her brother? She looked at Nicholas. His eyes telegraphed an appeal. Did he sense that she suspected the truth? She had only seconds in which to decide what to do. She didn't need that long. When Shane had allied himself with criminals, he had forfeited his right to her support.

"Thank you for defending my honor, *Your Highness,*" she said, emphasizing the title. "But I can fight my own battles."

Nicholas inclined his head in regal acknowledgment. "I don't doubt it."

"I was out of line about you being his mistress, Meagan," Shane said sullenly. "But what I said about him still goes. The royals use people."

Nicholas's jaw tightened. "And you don't?"

"I believe in everyone being equal."

"Yet you give orders to your sister and expect to have them obeyed."

"That's different."

Nicholas's head came up. "Is it? If you're all equal, why use threats against her child to get her to cooper-

ate? Surely Meagan should have the choice of partici-
pating in your scheme or not?"

Shane's grim look raked Meagan. "Seems you two
had quite a chat. Now it's my turn. Let's start with what
you know about the Chamber of Riches."

Nicholas gave a cool nod. "It won't take long. The
chamber is a myth, a product of fairy tale and legend."

"I grant you legends have sprung up around it,"
Shane agreed. "But the chamber itself is real."

"How can you be so sure?"

"Our source inside the castle said…" Shane broke
off, his expression turning sly. "Never mind how I
know. I just do."

He lifted his balled fist and Meagan saw Prince
Nicholas brace himself. She could stand it no longer.
"Shane, stop this. He's already told you he doesn't
know anything."

"Oh, I think he knows a lot more than he's telling us."
He leaned over Nicholas. "Will you tell me how to access
the chamber, or do I have to call Dave back in here?"

A lesser man might have cowered in the face of such
a threat, especially after suffering at Dave's hands once
before, but Nicholas drew himself up as far as his bonds
allowed. "Do what you like. I'll tell you nothing."

Her admiration for him was tempered by fear.
Whatever scheme Nicholas was hatching, she wished
he would act soon. She recognized that Shane's temper
was nearly at breaking point. She had to do something
before Nicholas provoked him beyond endurance and
paid the price.

She stood up, swaying slightly, her pallor all too genuine. "Shane, I…I feel terrible."

"What in the devil…?"

Meagan saw Nicholas start to lunge out of the chair, heard him cursing his bonds, then felt her brother catch her as she crumpled toward the floor.

She kept her eyes closed as she felt Shane place her on the sofa and drape a blanket over her. He chafed her hands in his. "Wake up, Meagan. Please wake up."

"Can't you see she's ill? All this is too much for her. Get her a doctor, man."

"I give the orders around here."

"Then give one to that hulking brute outside. Send him for help."

"You'd like that, wouldn't you? Sending my best man away would increase your chance of escaping."

"If I give you my word not to try to escape, will you send for a doctor?"

Meagan almost betrayed herself by opening her eyes. How could Nicholas make such a promise? She had staged her fainting spell precisely to give him the chance to make whatever move he had planned. Offering himself as a hostage for her defeated her purpose.

She gave a soft moan and allowed her eyes to flutter open. "What happened?"

Shane looked nonplussed. "You keeled over. I didn't know what to do."

"I told you what to do."

She looked up to find Nicholas on his feet, balancing awkwardly with his hands still tied behind him.

Why hadn't he done something? She lifted her head. "I'm all right now."

"You're not all right. You should see a doctor."

Nicholas's concern was almost her undoing. She felt her vision blur and blinked to clear it. "Really, I'm fine. I just need to rest."

Clumsily, Shane adjusted the blanket over her legs. "Then rest you shall. I'll finish my discussion with the prince later."

He stood up and hustled Nicholas out of the room. She closed her eyes as genuine exhaustion threatened to overtake her. She had bought Nicholas some time. What he did with it now was up to him.

Chapter Five

Trust his luck to have a jailer who read the tabloid, Ben thought. He was fairly sure Meagan suspected that he wasn't Prince Nicholas, and wished he knew whether or not her fainting spell yesterday had been a misguided attempt to help him.

Seeing her crumpling to the floor before Shane caught her had made Ben crazy. She had looked so helpless that he had wanted to snatch her from her brother and cradle her as tenderly as she deserved. For the first time since this started, he had truly felt like a captive. But not of Shane and his gang. Of a delicate beauty with a core of steel.

She was the last woman he should feel this way about, Ben thought. Living dangerously with no thought for her own safety, Meagan reminded him too much of his late fiancée, Marina. Letting himself care about her was asking for trouble.

If Meagan had tried to create a diversion, it had done more harm than good, landing Ben back in this tiny room, with another beating from Dave when he had resisted being tied up again.

Pain flamed around his wrists where he'd strained at the ropes. His ribs felt as if they'd been used as a trampoline. Standing on his feet, with only his hands tied, he could still have tackled Shane to get the information he needed. Instead Miss Reckless had intervened, and Ben was back where he started.

Of course, her fainting spell could have been genuine. Ignoring the pain, Ben strained at his bonds, tied more tightly today. He would give anything to know she was really all right.

Meagan looked up from the breakfast she was preparing as Shane came in. He frowned. "Should you be doing that?"

Making herself rest yesterday had been torture, but it had hindered Shane from questioning Nicholas. Better still, her brother hadn't argued when she'd suggested leaving Molly at her friend's place until Meagan felt better. "I have to do something or I'll go crazy," she insisted.

Her brother's hand closed over hers before she could pick up the plate she had been preparing for the prince. "I'll take that. Bread and coffee will do for our royal guest."

"It's no trouble," she said, fighting the disappointment that welled inside her at the thought that she might not see Nicholas this morning. She wanted to assure herself that he was unharmed. It had nothing to do with the way thoughts of him made her pulse race and warmth surge through her.

"Dave will take care of him," he repeated. "He did a good job dressing him in everyday clothes yesterday." He gave the peak of his old cap a jaunty tug. "Bet it's the first time his nibs has felt rough cloth against that pampered skin of his. Remind him he's no better than the rest of us."

She couldn't help reading more into Shane's words than she wanted to hear, and her heart did a painful back-flip. "Dave didn't hurt Nicholas, did he?"

"Why do you care? Don't bother, I know the answer. You always had a soft spot for the royal family, even when we were children."

"They've done a lot of good for us."

His lip twisted. "They've done a lot of good for themselves, but it's our turn now. You, me and Molly. Don't you want more for her than this?" His sweeping gesture took in their modest surroundings.

"Of course I do. But this isn't the way."

"It's the only way."

He took the plate she had prepared for Nicholas, and sat down at the kitchen table to eat. At a loss, she looked around then picked up the cast-iron coffeepot and two cups. "Is it all right if I take Dave some coffee?"

Shane nodded. "It'll help him wash away the taint of royalty."

She found Dave at the back door, staring out at the forest. He looked pale but when she asked if he was all right, he nodded without saying anything. Wisps of morning mist threaded between the trees. "It's going to be warm later," she said, pouring some of the coffee into one of the cups for him. He was so tall and broad-shouldered that she felt childlike beside him. Dave was about her age, but had spent so much time in and out of reform facilities that he had never gained much schooling. He spoke little and it had taken her weeks to discover that he had a speech impediment.

Dave accepted the coffee with an appreciative grunt, but she knew better than to expect much conversation. She tried anyway. "How is Nicholas this morning?"

As she'd hoped, the big man jerked his head toward Molly's bedroom. "S-See f-for yourself."

As if in no hurry, she moved down the hallway and pushed the bedroom door open. Nicholas was sitting up. Even she could see that he had been tied to the bedstead much more efficiently this time. His face was shadowed and looked gaunt. But he still looked regal and quite wonderful to her covert inspection.

When she tried to speak her throat felt dry. "Good morning, Your Highness."

He regarded her from under half-lowered lids. "I see you're fully recovered this morning."

She moved closer and drew a sharp breath. A

fresh bruise blossomed under his eye, and he moved carefully, as if his ribs pained him. "Are you all right?" she asked.

"I'll live, no thanks to your little performance yesterday."

"I have no idea what you mean."

"I'm sure you meant well, but as you can see, I was better off without the help. If I was suspicious of your fainting spell, chances are your brother was, too."

"At least it stopped Shane beating you to a pulp."

"How long do they intend keeping me prisoner?"

"As long as it takes to get the information we need," came a voice from behind Meagan.

Ben didn't miss the fear that invaded Meagan's eyes. "If it isn't the Grand Inquisitor," he drawled.

Shane ignored him, whirling on Meagan. "I'll teach you to side with him." He lifted his arm. She flinched away and Ben braced himself against the ropes, wishing the younger man would move within kicking distance. Shane saw the movement. "Don't like it when I threaten the lady, do you, Your Highness?" He made the title sound like an insult. "All you have to do is cooperate to protect her and the little girl."

"Only a coward threatens women and children," Ben snapped.

Shane looked as if he would like to hurl himself at Ben. "Sticks and stones," he said easily, but anger glittered in his gaze. "Your opinion doesn't count."

"Then why keep me alive?"

"Your dear daddy had a slight stroke," Shane said. "A

doctor says he'll be okay, but he's not talking too clearly right now. Seems he can't manage even one word."

Ben was careful not to reveal how much the news dismayed him. Meagan looked upset too, he saw. Ben was starting to believe she really was on his side. He was surprised at how much his spirits lifted at the notion. "Even if he could, King Michael wouldn't tell you anything you can use against the royal family," he said, masking his concern.

"There's only one thing I want to know, the password that will get me into the Chamber of Riches."

Ben kept his face impassive. Like every member of the royal family he had heard of the chamber's existence, but the details were known only to the monarch and the heir apparent. According to one legend, a password provided the key to a code contained within an ancient document. It supposedly told where to find a fresco on the outer wall of the chamber. If the fresco was pressed in a certain place and in a certain way, using an ancient ring worn by the king, one could gain access to the chamber.

Ben wasn't sure he believed the stories, although he'd seen a ring that fitted the legend, worn by King Michael. Shane's people must have gained possession of the ring, and now wanted to put it to the test. If there was a password, Ben certainly didn't know it. "I told you yesterday, the chamber is a myth," he said, hoping this wasn't the end of the line for his charade.

"His kingship disagrees," Shane said. "Before he had the stroke, he confirmed that the chamber does exist."

Ben could only imagine at what cost. "Then you also know that he hasn't told me the password yet." Ben could only pray it tallied with what the conspirators already knew.

"Wrong answer. From King Michael and…well from various sources, we're convinced that Nicholas *does* know the password. So either you're playing dumb, or…" he moved to the side of the bed, his expression menacing "…you're not Nicholas Stanbury."

Ben heard Meagan's indrawn breath, hastily stifled. She knew, he thought. Somehow she had worked it out. It came to him that she might have betrayed him, and hadn't. The thought was surprisingly comforting. With Shane, he decided to try to bluff it out. "That's ridiculous."

"Is it, Your Highness? If you *are* anybody's highness."

"Who else would I be?" Just a few more inches closer, Ben willed as he saw Shane's anger overwhelm his caution.

"The king's cousin," Meagan whispered. She had been right after all.

Shane's surprised look at Meagan provided the distraction Ben needed. His hands were gripping the ropes and he used them as leverage while he brought his legs up against his chest then shot them forward to impact against Shane's chest. The other man went down as if poleaxed, striking his head against the dresser as he fell.

"Wh-what's g-going on?" The giant, Dave, bolted through the door, coming up short at the sight of Shane lying unconscious on the floor. With a cry of anger, he lunged at Ben.

Meagan didn't stop to think. She hefted the coffee-pot and brought it down on the back of Dave's head. With a moan he also collapsed, coffee streaming down his back. She stared at the fallen man, transfixed.

Ben saw she was verging on shock. "We have to get out of here, now," he said in the command tone his men would have recognized and obeyed instantly.

She wasn't under his command, but it worked. Her slightly glazed look was replaced by fear overlaid with determination. "You're right. I'll untie you."

Ben had begun working on the ropes, and had one hand free before she reached him. He could have finished the job more quickly himself, but he let her fumble with the other rope, sensing that she needed the activity while she dealt with what she had just done.

He suspected she hadn't had to knock anyone unconscious before. He hadn't made a habit of it either, but it was only because he believed in taking preventive action. His first commanding officer, Mike Stafford, had rammed the lesson home to him one night in a bar on the other side of the world after a bunch of rowdies tried to provoke them into a fight. Ben would have obliged them, but Mike had shown him a better way. By his aggressive stance and unyielding confidence, he had projected that he was the alpha male here.

The display had worked. The rowdies had slunk away, hurling taunts as they went. It was the first time Ben had won a fight without so much as throwing a punch, but it wasn't the last. He had used Mike's trick several times, and the aggressors had backed off every time. Until now.

"I'm sorry about your brother," he said, as she freed his hand at last. He massaged his raw wrists, flexing his fingers to regain full feeling.

"It was his own fault," she said, sounding hurt. "Why did you pretend to be the prince?"

"So your brother's people would do exactly what they did, and, we hoped, lead me to where they're holding King Michael." Levering himself to his feet, he rested a hand on her shoulder and used the other to tilt her face up to his. "The real Prince Nicholas is in a safe hiding place. I couldn't risk telling you the truth."

He felt the tension in her lithe body as she affected a shrug. "I'm used to men misleading me."

She didn't add, "You're no different than the rest," although he heard it anyway and wondered who had given her such a warped view of the male of the species. Later would do to try to change her preconceptions, he decided, wondering why he should want to. "I meant it, we must get out of here," he said crisply. "You're coming with me."

"To the castle?"

He shook his head. "Since Shane let it slip that they have a contact on the inside, I won't risk it." *I won't risk you,* came the thought, but he kept it to himself.

She shook her head. "This is my home. I'm staying here."

"When Shane and Dave wake up, they'll want

revenge." He played the trump card. "Think of Molly. I know somewhere you'll both be safe."

He had said the one thing guaranteed to gain her cooperation. "Very well. We'll take my car. It isn't what you're used to but…"

He turned her to look at him again. "I'm not the prince, remember? My name is Lieutenant Ben Lockhart, Edenbourg Royal Navy. But then you already suspected who I was, didn't you? That's why you pulled your fainting stunt."

She stared at him. "How did you know?"

"Lucky guess. And thanks. But if you ever stick your neck out again on my account, I vow I'll wring it for you."

She masked her hurt with annoyance. "I couldn't let my brother hurt you."

"I could have handled him. By double-crossing Shane, you put yourself in danger. I want your word there'll be no more heroics."

"I'm not answerable to you. Unless you're pulling royal rank." Strange how the thought troubled her.

"Rank doesn't come into this. Your word, Meagan."

Molly's safety depended on him, so Meagan nodded, seething. He may not believe in royal rank, but she gathered that gender was another matter. "I'll be a good little woman, I promise."

"That attitude won't get you anywhere but killed." She winced, and his tone softened. "Do you need to take anything with you?"

"Raggedy-May," she said, picking up the doll. "Molly was fretting for her last night."

"My cousin, Princess Isabel, used to like the Raggedy-May stories," he told her as he hurried her out of the room. "Isabel preferred to play the intrepid scarecrow, Strawbie. She used to rewrite the scenarios so we had two Strawbies, making for some conflict over the chain of command. Some things never change."

"You've made your point," Meagan snapped. As they passed her bedroom, she ducked in and grabbed her purse then glanced around. "What about clothes?"

A low moan coming from Molly's room alerted Ben. "There's no time. We can buy whatever you need on the way. We're getting out of here now."

"What about the men in the forest?"

Ben loped back to Molly's room and returned wearing Shane's baseball cap. "Do you think I'll pass for your brother?"

The homespun clothes and cap helped, but didn't disguise Ben's military bearing. She was glad that her car was parked in shadow beside the house, but they would need to pray that none of the men took a close look at them as they drove off. "Only if we move quickly," she said.

He nodded. "Exactly what I had in mind."

Chapter Six

In the back of Meagan's car, Molly bounced up and down in the child safety seat. At first she had been wary of Ben when he and Meagan had arrived at Anna Carmody's place to collect her, but the child had quickly warmed to his gentle manner.

He was good with children, Meagan thought. He had dropped down to Molly's level to explain that he was taking her mummy on a special holiday, and would deem it an honor if she came, too. Molly had giggled and asked where they were going. When Ben said "the seaside," the three-year-old had been totally won over.

Like Anna, Meagan thought. In the face of Ben's unassuming charm, Anna had practically melted. Meagan hadn't been able to convince her that she wasn't witnessing a budding romance. Since telling Anna the truth might put her in danger, Meagan was forced to let her think what she would.

"Look, Mummy, a big pond," the three-year-old exclaimed, pointing to the sea spread out in front of them.

Ben smiled. "That's the ocean, little one. It's the biggest pond there is."

His tone, warm and faintly nostalgic, caught Meagan's attention. "You love it, don't you?"

Steering the car along the narrow road that twisted down toward the coast, he nodded. "At sea you get a sense of what's really important. There are no borders between countries or people."

"Did you join the navy because you love the sea?"

He shook his head. "I've always loved sailing, but resisted making it a career, probably because it was what my father wanted. At the time, I would do almost anything he disapproved of, as a way of asserting myself, not realizing this made me as pig-headed as he was, and therefore just like him, until it came down to a couple of fairly basic choices, and the navy was the best of them."

"The other being royal life, I suppose."

She glanced over at him and saw his mouth twist. "Nothing so noble."

"Then what?"

"Reform school."

"Reform school? You?" She knew her tone reflected her disbelief.

His hands tightened around the wheel. "Your

brother wasn't the only one with an identity crisis, or a need to bend the world to his will."

"That's quite a summing-up, considering you knew Shane so briefly, under such dreadful circumstances."

"In some ways, meeting him was like seeing myself when I was a teenager."

"But Shane was an orphan. He had no idea where he fitted in. But I suppose he never really grew up."

"There's more than one kind of orphan."

She had difficulty imagining Ben as a rebel. "You're saying you didn't know where you fitted in, either?"

"Having one parent who is a princess, up to her ears in royal duties, and another who's navy-tough, and at sea most of the time, doesn't make life easy. I spent more time with their staff than with my parents. At court I was 'the navy brat,' and around my father's friends I was 'the little prince.'"

"So in the end, you didn't know what you were."

He flashed her an icy look. "No need to sound so tragic. I wasn't cold, I wasn't hungry, and although I didn't know it at the time, I was loved."

"But you were caught between two worlds, belonging in neither."

He nodded tautly. "No matter how I felt, I wasn't entitled to hang out with the wrong crowd, or take stupid risks, not always the legal kind."

He had obviously straightened himself out somehow. "So what changed you?"

"I was hauled home by the constabulary when my dad happened to be home on leave. He gave me a choice between following him into the navy or letting the law take care of me. Not surprisingly, I chose the navy."

"And found your spiritual home."

He shot her a wry grin. "Nothing so fancy or quick. During training I carried a chip the size of Edenbourg on my shoulder, until I met a man who not only thought he was tougher than me, he was. He taught me a thing or two about life, and my place in it. You're about to meet him."

She frowned, not sure she was ready for the kind of closeness his announcement implied. This man, whoever he was, was obviously important to Ben still. "I thought you were taking us to a royal hideaway."

He gave her a look of satisfaction. "I am. Mine."

She barely had time to digest this before they rounded a final bend. Spread out before them was a fishing village that looked as if it hadn't changed since the eighteenth century. Ancient stone houses with slate-tiled roofs crowded the rim of a long, narrow estuary where tall sailing ships rode at anchor on a ribbon of black water.

She gasped in admiration. "It's beautiful."

"According to local lore, Eden Cove was a thriving shipping port for centuries, until a fisherman caught what he thought was a seal at the estuary mouth. Instead he had captured a mermaid called Enid who cursed the estuary, promising many lives would be lost there. Unfortunately, many were. They came to grief on a sand bar known as the Doom Bar, said to have been conjured up by the mermaid's father. It's long been dredged clear, although the two headlands are still called Doom Bar and Enid's Landing."

"Mermaids and curses, it sounds impossibly romantic." Not a place she had any business being with Ben, she thought. "Are you sure this is necessary?"

"Safer than going to the castle until I have more clues to the identity of Shane's informer."

Molly's eyes were as round as saucers as she took in all the new sights. "Sea girls, Mummy! Look at all the sea girls."

"Gulls, sweetheart," Meagan corrected automatically, wishing she shared Molly's innocent excitement. She felt apprehensive, wondering what she had agreed to by allowing Ben to bring them here. It was obviously special to him, and the man he had hinted she would meet was important in his life. She hadn't planned on getting that involved with him.

Involved? She almost laughed aloud. Did she have a choice? When Shane came around, he would be after Ben's blood. Hers too, now that she had made her allegiance clear. The thought of what he might do to Molly made her blood run cold. Unconsciously she moved closer to Ben, reassured by his closeness. She might find his macho attitude offputting, but he inspired her confidence and trust.

From the moment she first saw him, she had been drawn to him by forces beyond her control. The pull was more than physical, although there was enough of that to swamp her defenses. There was also courage, compassion and a heart the size of the castle. He had willingly put his life at risk for king and country, and now he was doing it for her and Molly.

A tidal wave of longing raged through Meagan, as potent as it was futile. For the first time, she understood Shane's craving to be other than who he was. She felt it now, knowing Ben was the cause. But as long as he insisted that she play the lesser role of "little woman" they wouldn't get anywhere.

"We're here."

The tall house on the rim of the bay was ancient, cared-for and unmistakably Ben's. His touch was in every room he showed her, not only in the collection of old sailing artifacts that adorned the walls, but in the order she saw everywhere.

"Now I know what's meant by shipshape," she said. A good-looking woman in her fifties emerged from the kitchen, wiping floury hands on an apron. Meagan gave an involuntary start.

Ben dropped an arm around her shoulders. "Relax, it's only my housekeeper."

"I'm Hannah Gordon, ma'am. Lieutenant Lockhart called to let me know you were on the way. Everything's ready for you."

So that's who Ben had called soon after leaving the cottage. They had stopped to allow Meagan to buy a few things Molly needed. Ben had no money on him, and couldn't risk going to the bank for fear of leaving a paper trail that tipped the conspirators off as to their whereabouts. Fortunately, Meagan had recently been paid in cash for a dressmaking job, and hadn't had a chance to go to the bank herself. The extra spending wouldn't help her budget, but she had no alternative.

She shook the housekeeper's hand. "I'm Meagan Moore. This is my daughter, Molly."

Hannah turned to Molly. "How old are you, sweetheart?"

Molly held up three fingers. Hannah looked at the rag doll clutched in Molly's arms. "Such a big girl. Probably too big for all the Raggedy-May and Strawbie stories I happen to know."

Molly's small face puckered. "I'm not too big, am I, Mummy?"

"Definitely not." Molly's answering smile tugged at Meagan's heartstrings. She blessed Ben silently for his choice of housekeeper. This situation was tough enough on her child. Anyone who made things easier for Molly had Meagan's heartfelt gratitude.

Hannah broke into her thoughts. "I'll show you to your rooms so you can rest."

"Molly needs a nap, but I'm fine." Meagan was too edgy to think of resting. It was all she could do not to keep looking over her shoulder. Ben had assured her they were safe, choosing a roundabout route and doubling back several times to thwart any attempt at pursuit. Nevertheless Meagan's nerves felt stretched almost to the breaking point.

"Would you prefer to take a walk?" Ben asked, noticing her restlessness.

She looked at Molly. "Is it safe?"

"The house may be old but the security system is

state-of-the-art. Molly will be fine with Hannah, and you'll be with me."

Meagan felt a blush starting and willed it away. She would *not* read anything into his assurance, tempting though it was. "Then I'd like to walk."

While Hannah hovered nearby, Meagan tucked Molly up in bed with her rag doll, in a delightful attic room under the eaves of the old house. The little girl smiled sleepily. "Raggedy-May likes it here."

The doll wasn't the only one, Meagan thought. She hadn't known how much she'd been living on her nerves the last few days, until she'd stopped. "I like it here, too," she whispered as she kissed Molly.

"Can we stay?"

"For a little while." Forever, argued Meagan's heart. She felt herself sinking again. "Look after Hannah."

Molly giggled. "No, Mummy. She's going to look after me."

Who would look after *her?* Meagan wondered as she set off with Ben. It felt odd to be taken under his wing, but comforting. Too comforting. She had a constant battle to remember that she was with him only for protection. As soon as he could contact the castle without alerting Shane's informer, Ben would make other arrangements for her and Molly and return to his own life.

She was aware that Ben was trying to put her at ease by explaining the town's history and pointing out landmarks. But she jumped at every sudden noise and after a short time, he pulled her into the shadow of a building. "Relax, no harm will come to you here."

"Unless Shane's people find us."

"They won't. But if it will make you feel better, we'll get out of sight."

She had expected him to take her back to his house, but he brought her to the dock and helped her to board a square-rigged sailing vessel riding at anchor there.

"Welcome aboard *Pathfinder,*" he said, "the navy's sailing-training vessel."

The ship was deserted for now, but with her back to the cove she could feel transported to the eighteenth century when the deck would have swarmed with brigands and pirates. "It's very impressive. Did you train aboard here?"

"I wouldn't let His Highness near the rigging," boomed a gravelly voice.

A pulse leaped in her throat, but when she spun around, she found a uniformed man bearing down on them. He was almost as wide as he was tall. Ben stepped between them. "This is Captain Mike Stafford, master of *Pathfinder.* Mike, my guest, Meagan Moore."

The captain looked intrigued. "Consider yourself flattered. Ben doesn't bring many ladies aboard this ship."

She felt herself redden, annoyed to find she was pleased. "I hope you don't mind me coming aboard."

"Feel free to look around. I'll be in the great cabin if you need me."

"Great cabin?" she asked Ben after the captain had gone below.

"A kind of captain's office and mess in one."

"I see."

She felt awkward suddenly, out of place. Ben, on the other hand, looked at home riding the shifting deck with the ease of long experience. He didn't even notice he was doing it, so at home was he in the masculine environment. She felt the gulf between them widen. "Why have a replica seventeenth-century ship in a modern navy?" she asked.

"Nothing gives you more of a sense of oneness with the sea than making passage under sail," Ben explained. "As well as seamanship, the cadets and the civilian teenagers who train aboard her gain skills, confidence and self-esteem."

She thought of what he had told her about his own teenage years. "All the qualities you had to learn the hard way."

"My father thought it was the best way, but it isn't."

"No, it isn't." She had also learned her lessons through bitter experience, and wouldn't recommend it to anyone. "Mike seems nice under all that gruffness."

"He'd be disappointed you spotted it, but you're right."

The warmth in his voice alerted her. "He's the former commanding officer you talked about."

Ben nodded. "Retired now. This is a voluntary post, but I'd like to see anyone try and take it away from him."

"The trainees are very lucky."

"Would you like to see below?"

Since the alternative was to remain above decks, where she felt uncomfortably vulnerable, she nodded agreement. She regretted it when she found how often he had to help her down ladders—companionways, as he called them—every touch of skin to skin searing her like a brand. It was difficult to concentrate as he showed her through a maze of cabins, reeling off names like sailroom, chartroom, and firehearth, till they reached the crew's mess deck.

Dodging swinging hammocks, she protested, "Time out, please. All this climbing is exhausting." Not to mention the strain of keeping her response to him in check.

He guided her to a hammock and steadied it while she sat on the edge, her feet barely touching the deck. "You can rest for a moment here."

She wriggled her feet free of her shoes. "Eden Cove is one of the kingdom's best-kept secrets."

"Exactly why I made a home here."

"Home," she mused. "I've never really known where home is for me."

"You have your cottage."

She had loved it because it was hers, but knew she would never feel the same way about it again after all that had happened there. "I may not stay," she said, knowing she wouldn't.

"Where will you go?"

"I don't know. It scares me a little." It scared her a lot, but pride stopped her from telling him so.

"You could have a place at the castle," he said carefully. "My aunt has been looking for someone as skilled with a needle as you appear to be."

Being offered a royal appointment would be the answer to a prayer, but it would also mean never being free of Ben. She would be on the sidelines when he visited his family, hearing the gossip when he came to seek the queen's blessing for his marriage. Perhaps she would be expected to sew for the wedding party. A lump filled her throat. "I don't think so."

"Are you refusing to consider it on my account?"

Her wide-eyed gaze flew to his face. "Why do you ask?"

"Because you feel it, too."

She shook her head in violent denial. "There's nothing to feel." Nothing she would allow herself as long as he treated her like a hothouse flower instead of an equal.

He looked savage. "Then explain why you tremble when I touch you? Not with fear. When I look into your eyes, I see the same primitive need that's ripping me to shreds. We have to do something about it."

She knew what the something would be. They would make love, then their different beliefs would drive them apart. "I've told you I can't."

"Because of Molly's father." It wasn't a question. "You'd deny what's between us because of loyalty to a man who'd leave you for another?"

Anger drove her to her feet but she didn't allow for the unpredictable movement of the hammock. She would have tumbled backward, but for Ben's lightning reflexes.

As his hands clamped around her she twisted in his grasp, confused between anger and a burgeoning sense of pleasure so hot and sweet that she felt ashamed of herself for feeling it. "Molly's father didn't leave me for anyone else. He was already married. I just didn't know it. Let me go."

"Not until you see sense. You can't waste your life waiting for a man who isn't worthy of your love."

"Love doesn't come into it." Not the way it kept doing with Ben.

He frowned. "You don't love him. You don't care that he was married. What's going on, Meagan?"

"Nothing you would understand."

"I'm beginning to. He hurt you, didn't he? That's why you're fighting me so hard. You're afraid it will happen again."

"I promised myself I wouldn't let it." Her voice came out as a strained whisper.

He brushed the hair back from her face. "And now?"

"Now I can't seem to stop it."

"You don't have to. All you have to do is accept it."

If she did, she was lost. "You make it sound simple." It probably was, for him. "It isn't so easy for me."

"Because?"

"You aren't offering me forever, any more than Kevan did."

His gaze smoldered. "We both know there's no such thing as forever. It's no reason to lump me in with a heartless brute who could give you his child then abandon you." His hold tightened as he voiced a sudden suspicion. "Is he threatening you to keep your loyalty?"

"He isn't threatening me. He isn't around anymore," she said, wishing she could tell Ben the truth, that

Kevan had left for good soon after Molly was conceived. But it would make her even more vulnerable to Ben himself.

"Yet you still love him. Why?"

"It doesn't matter."

"It does to me. I need to know how you can still love him, yet respond so to me."

Denial was the only defense she had left. "You're wrong."

"Am I wrong about your reaction when I touch you? When I do this?" His mouth crushed hers, merciless in demanding a response from her. She couldn't withhold it any more than she could stop herself from returning the pressure, as greedy as she was to taste him, to feel the pressure of flesh against flesh, heat meeting heat.

The cabin tilted around her as he lowered her into the hammock, dropping to one knee beside her to caress and explore. The hammock's motion made her feel disoriented, free-floating, as if she was suspended in time and space. Unable to stop herself, she returned his kisses with all the passion at her command, drawing dizzying lungfuls of air as he undid the top button of her shirt and stroked the warm fullness within.

Tearing himself away from her, he closed the cabin door then came back to her side. "Great oceans, Meagan. Do you know what you do to me?"

Exactly what he did to her, she suspected. He made her want the moon and the stars, and worse, made them seem within her grasp. It wasn't true, but she couldn't bring herself to end this, not yet. Having his mouth on hers and his body heat searing through her was too intoxicating.

She slid her hands under his shirt, wanting to touch, to know everything. Beautiful, hard-muscled chest, the corrugation of ribs, the palm-teasing abrasiveness of male hair and skin, lower and lower until she heard his breath catch.

She had become so lost in exploring that she hadn't thought ahead. Quickly she pulled her hands away. But he took them in his, kissed her fingertips and placed them low on his ribs again. "You know I want you."

Her hands stilled as fear gripped her. "I want you too, but…"

His finger against her lips silenced her. "No buts. I'm not Kevan."

He couldn't be. Kevan had taken what he wanted by fair means or otherwise. Ben would never manipulate her to get his own way. Even now with desire carving lines of strain into his face, he was waiting for her. "I know."

"Then you know I would never deliberately hurt you."

He wouldn't mean to, but he would hurt her. Wanting her wasn't the same as loving her. Knowing it didn't stop madness from gripping her. "Oh, Ben."

It was all the invitation he needed. He gathered her against him, skimming his mouth against her hairline, and along the side of her face to her breasts. Heat powered through her. She answered it by tangling her fingers in his hair and pulling his head up to claim his mouth in a kiss driven by the force of her own desire.

He tried to slide into the hammock beside her, but the swaying motion defeated him. With a groan, he stood up, taking her hands. "We have to find a bunk that will stay still."

She hesitated. "I can't. I'm sorry."

He took her hands. "Am I going too fast?"

"We both are." The hectic color she felt in her cheeks and the pounding of her heart denied that it was one-sided. She tried to be glad of the reprieve but couldn't. Not when she felt so achingly bereft. She had wanted him so. Still wanted him with every breath in her.

When he reached for the buttons of her shirt she shook her head. "I'll do it." If he so much as touched her, she was lost, so fragile was her self-control.

"I'll be…up on deck."

He swung himself through the door and she heard his footsteps retreating as he made his way topside. She took a minute to steady her breathing, then tidied her clothing, knowing it would take much longer to restore her peace of mind.

How could she have been so stupid? By admitting that Kevan was gone, she had demolished the last barrier between her and Ben. She may as well have invited him into her bed because they would end up there. She knew it as well as her own name.

Chapter Seven

Plunging into the maze of passageways outside the cabin, Meagan quickly lost her bearings and almost ran into Captain Stafford coming the other way. He steadied her then took a look at her flushed features. "Are you okay?"

His wise eyes looked as if they saw more than she wanted him to. "I'm fine. I got lost looking for Ben."

"He's climbing a tall mast. Said it's as good as a cold shower. I'm starting to understand what he meant."

The captain opened a door into a large room littered with charts. This must be the great cabin Ben had told her about. "Join me for coffee."

"Shouldn't I find Ben?"

Mike put a steaming mug of coffee in front of her,

pushing cream and sugar toward her. "He's best left alone for the moment. You look as if you could use some time out yourself."

It was true. She cupped her hands around the mug, grateful for its warmth. "Ben's a complicated man."

"Most people are complicated. At least his is the good kind."

She looked at him through a curling haze of steam. "Care to explain that?"

He chuckled. "Forthright, I like that in a woman. So does Ben."

"He hides it well." She explained about Ben's refusal to accept her as an equal. "Is it me, or all women?"

The captain seemed to weigh up the wisdom of answering her. "If Ben acts overly protectively, it's because he was hurt very badly when his fiancée was killed."

"He was engaged to be married?"

"To Marina, another naval officer. She was killed when they served on a peace-keeping mission together."

Meagan's breath caught in her throat. "Was he unable to protect her?" It would explain a lot.

"Worse. He thinks if he hadn't been the one handing out the assignments, she wouldn't have died."

Compassion for Ben flooded through her. "He sent her on the mission?" she asked softly.

"The opposite. She'd had a virus and he ordered her to stand down because he thought she wasn't fully recovered."

She felt a frown gather. "Then how can he blame himself?"

"She was determined to show him she could handle it, and took another officer's place. Ben thinks if he hadn't tried to stop her, she wouldn't have behaved so recklessly."

"What do you think?"

"She wasn't fit. She froze at a crucial moment." He stirred his coffee thoughtfully. "After she died, Ben buried himself in his work. I thought he'd stay a bachelor like me, wedded to the navy." He got up and paced. "Don't get me wrong, it's a good life. But a man needs more. From the way he looks at you, I was wondering if you might be the more."

Meagan sipped her coffee, wincing at its strength. The feelings flooding through her at Mike's suggestion were stronger still. "He doesn't want more. After Marina, the last thing he wants is commitment."

"You think Ben is avoiding commitment?"

"After what you've just told me, it would be understandable."

He gestured around. "Shows what you know. *Pathfinder* is the biggest commitment going, yet Ben took it on."

"He told me this vessel provides sailing experience for troubled teenagers. Doesn't it belong to the navy?"

"It's on permanent loan. Ben owns it and funds the project himself."

She set the mug down. "But how?"

"As Princess Karenna's son, he became Duke of Norbourg with the attendant property and income when he turned twenty-one. He gives all the income to the project while he lives on his navy salary. Nobody's supposed to know he does it, but I think you should. Might help to understand him better."

For all the good it would do her. "I know he's a generous man. It doesn't change his attitude toward women in general and me in particular."

The captain stroked his neatly trimmed beard. "Ben's capable of change. If anyone knows that, it's me. You should have seen him when he first came under my command."

"He credits you with teaching him a lot about life."

Mike shook his head. "All I did was teach him to accept who he is, and show him he can make his own place in the world."

It was a lesson many people never learned. She guessed that Mike underestimated his role in Ben's life. "All the same, he's not likely to risk another relationship."

"Have you considered he might simply be careful what commitments he chooses to make?"

Mike Stafford's message became clear. If Ben could commit so much of himself to helping young people he didn't know, perhaps she was being hasty in judging him. She stood up. "I'd better find him."

The captain looked pleased. "That's more like it. I always say navy coffee can cure anything."

She smiled, sharing Ben's liking for his old commanding officer. "This is going to take more than coffee, but it's a start."

At thirty meters aloft the wind was a primal force

trying to tear Ben from the rigging. He edged out along the wooden spar, training and experience keeping his weight up and over the yard, and his feet from skidding on the foot ropes. If *Pathfinder* had been at sea, he would be fighting a mix of wind, waves and flapping canvas, as well.

Today he had only himself to fight as he inched his way outward, needing the momentum of action to dispel his frustration. It wasn't only sexual, although Meagan was beautiful and desirable enough to arouse any man. But there was more going on here, and he wasn't sure what to call it, far less how to deal with it.

"Look outward, stay focused," Mike Stafford had drummed into him when he was a raw recruit. How did a man stay focused with a woman like Meagan getting under his skin despite his efforts to prevent it?

She deserved more than he was prepared to give. They both knew Ben didn't believe in happy endings. At least he thought he hadn't until she came along. Now he wasn't sure anymore, and he hated the feeling. It reminded him too much of when he was caught between two worlds, belonging in neither. He preferred certainty.

He knew what Mike would say. "Nothing's certain in life except the wind and the tides." But what about love? Just thinking the word was enough to leave Ben dangling from the yard.

He regained his balance in time to see Meagan come onto the weather deck, her glorious hair streaming in the wind as she looked around. He felt like a fool. He hadn't wanted her to see the effect she had on him, but climbing the rigging had been instinctive, as was his gut reaction at the sight of her. Against all common sense, he wanted her more than he had ever wanted any woman.

He climbed down carefully. She came to him, dodging the binnacles and ropes cluttering the deck, and he was struck again by how beautiful she was. His stomach clenched and he felt overheated, knowing better than to blame the arduous climb. Only as she reached him did he see that her face was white. "What is it?"

"It's Molly. Captain Stafford just got a call from Hannah. She guessed you might be here. Oh, Ben, Molly's missing."

He was moving as he spoke. "How long?"

She struggled to keep pace, and he took her arm to help her negotiate the coiled lines and gear strewing the deck. "Less than an hour. She was gone when Hannah checked on her during her nap." She clutched his hand. "I should have stayed with her."

He heard the self-condemnation in her voice. "It won't help to blame yourself. She can't be far."

"Unless the conspirators have taken her as a way to get back at us. Shane always said she'd be the one to suffer if I crossed him."

Ben turned her to face him, wanting to take her in his arms and kiss her until he drove out the fear, but he kept his touch reassuring. "Listen to me. She may have been confused by the strange surroundings, and wandered off. But if she has been taken, we'll find her. Either way, you'll get her back, I promise."

Meagan drew strength from his confidence, wanting to trust him. It was unnerving, putting her faith in him after relying on herself for so long, but she sensed that if anyone could bring Molly back safely, he could. She had seen enough to know he cared about the little girl.

Hannah was white-faced and pacing up and down, when they joined her at the house. "She was asleep when I went to unpack Miss Moore's things. Then when I went back to check, she was gone."

"Stop this, nobody's blaming you," Ben snapped in a command tone. Hannah became visibly calmer. "Now tell me where you've searched."

She explained that she had scoured the house from top to bottom, and had begun to check the grounds when Ben returned. "I'll finish out there," Ben said. "You stay by the phone."

The implication that there might be a ransom demand or threat chilled Meagan's blood, threatening to paralyze her, but she fought it. Ben could be right. Molly could simply have wandered off. "I'll check out front," Meagan said.

"We'll meet out back in five minutes."

They were the longest five minutes of Meagan's life. It didn't take her long to search the compact front garden. Then she went out into the cobbled street, calling Molly's name, growing steadily more terrified when no answer came.

If Shane's people had found them somehow, Meagan knew she would never forgive herself. How could she have lost herself in Ben's arms, even for a moment, while her child was in danger? If she could only have Molly back safely, this would never happen again, Meagan promised herself.

Ben's voice penetrated her terror. "It's all right, I've found her."

Meagan raced around the side of the house, following Ben's voice to the former coachhouse now serving as a garage. A small door opened in the bottom of the massive main door. She went through at a crouching run, then straightened to find her daughter cradled against Ben's broad chest. Molly's head rested against his shoulder and one tiny hand clutched the front of his shirt. The other gripped Mr. Snug by the leg.

Meagan's heart did a back-flip. Molly was all right. She was safe. Ben had kept his promise. Heart pounding, she went to them and stroked her baby's hair, keeping her voice low although Ben had to hear the tremor in it. "Where were you, sweetheart? Mummy was so worried."

Molly stuck a thumb into her mouth. Over the blond curls, Ben said, "She woke up and missed her teddy bear, then must have remembered she'd left it in the car and came looking for it. I found her in the back seat, fast asleep."

"What made you think to look in the car?"

"A hunch. I remembered seeing her with the doll, but not Mr. Snug."

He had remembered how important both toys were to Molly. Watching him talk to the little girl to reassure her, Meagan felt her chest tighten until it could barely contain her overflowing heart. She was emotionally vulnerable right now, but she also knew beyond a shadow of doubt that she was close to falling in love with Ben.

When had she crossed the line? Having a man care as much about her child as she did was a powerful aphrodisiac, but there was much more.

It was Ben himself. She had never known anyone who cared as much as he did. About his family, his country, his work, young people in need. He'd brought her and Molly here because he cared. It wasn't only physical, although his kisses took her breath away. She had only to remember how close they had come to making love aboard *Pathfinder.* If the stupid hammock had held still…thinking about it was enough to make her head spin.

At the same time, old fears swirled to the surface, warring with the pleasure. She couldn't afford to let herself feel this way. There were consequences. The child in Ben's arms was proof. Just because Shane's people hadn't taken Molly this time, didn't mean he wouldn't track them down and harm her child. Meagan vowed not to seek the comfort of Ben's arms again as long as Molly was in danger, but knew it would be a painful promise to keep.

Molly opened her fist to show Ben a tiny star-shaped object. "Look. Pretty button."

Ben traded a concerned look with Meagan. "Can I see it?"

Trustingly, the child surrendered the object. Ben studied it, frowning. "Looks like a surveillance device to me. It must have been hidden in the baby seat."

Meagan set her own turmoil aside. "Are you saying someone bugged my car?"

He nodded grimly, and fear fisted around her heart. "Who would have put it there?"

He didn't have to answer. "Shane. He didn't trust me to cooperate, so he took precautions."

Molly made a grab for the device. "Want my button."

Ben hugged Molly. "Hannah has much prettier buttons than this old thing. Shall we go and ask her?"

"Yes, please." Molly linked her chubby hands around his neck. They looked so natural together that Meagan could hardly bear it. Not even with Shane had her child been so trusting. The feeling was mutual, she saw as he carried Molly into the house, paying close attention to her chatter.

Although he reassured her that nobody blamed her, Hannah looked near tears and vowed over and over that she wouldn't let the child out of her sight again. At Ben's request she got out a jar of buttons, and sat down beside Molly as she began to sort them. Distracted, Molly didn't protest when Ben pocketed the star-shaped one.

Watching the little girl play, Ben said, "At the castle, a team of investigators is working on the kidnappings. I'll have to get this device to their commander, Adam Sinclair. It may be a vital clue."

"I thought it wasn't safe to return to the castle?"

Ben juggled the device in his palm. "Right now we're between a rock and a hard place. The conspirators know where you are. I can protect you more readily in a secure environment, so the castle it is."

He went to a well-stocked bar and poured two glasses of brandy, handing one to Meagan. When she protested that she didn't like spirits, he said, "You've had a shock. It will help calm you down."

She took a gulp, felt herself turn beet red. The fire was followed by a spreading sensation of warmth. She put the glass down. "I've never been so scared in my life."

His jaw tightened. "This has got to end."

Exactly what she had been thinking, although she knew he meant the situation with the missing King Michael. "Edward is doing a good job filling in for the king, isn't he?" she asked, forcing herself to focus on the situation. Bad as it was, it was more clear-cut than her turbulent feelings for Ben.

A frown of concern darkened Ben's features, making Meagan ache to smooth it away. She linked her hands to keep them still as Ben said, "He's doing his best to fill Michael's shoes, but Edward isn't up to it. He's been living in America for so long that he's out of touch. It would be easier if Prince Nicholas could return from the secret location, but his life would be in danger."

It was all so complicated. Fleetingly Meagan found herself longing for the simplicity of life with Molly and her work as a dressmaker. If Shane had understood the difficulties and strictures of royal life, would her brother have been so envious? From Ben she had gathered that it wasn't all ease and privilege and people bowing before you. The responsibilities weighed heavily as well as the dangers.

Thinking of Ben in jeopardy, Meagan felt her throat threaten to close. She looked at him, seated in a chair opposite her, vigilant even in relaxation. His long fingers curled around his drink, making her recall how they'd felt curled around her arms. How his generous mouth had moved over hers, eliciting responses she was powerless to withhold.

She took another cautious sip of brandy, deciding to redirect her thoughts before they got completely out of hand. "Mike Stafford told me about the *Pathfinder* project being your baby."

Ben's features wrinkled in annoyance. "Mike has a big mouth."

She set her drink aside. She didn't mention why Mike had felt the need to tell her Ben's secret. "He also has a big heart. He cares about you."

His shoulders lifted slightly. "I've known that for a long time."

"Why didn't you tell me you financed the project out of your own funds?"

He straightened. "What difference does it make?"

She kept her gaze on her linked fingers. "More than you think. It tells me you're not wary of commitment at all."

He stood up, looming over her. "And now you've discovered that I'm a closet philanthropist, and everything is clear, is that what you're going to tell me?"

Shocked understanding gripped her. He didn't know that her feelings for him were so strong that they were scaring her. Easier to justify walking away for her own survival, when she thought he wouldn't commit to anything lasting. Finding that he had another, caring side changed the rules. He was more than willing to commit if his heart was in it.

So his heart wasn't in anything more than a casual fling with her. He was no different from Kevan after all. Kevan had hidden behind his marriage, and Ben had decided that she was a reckless opportunist. It wasn't true. She hadn't cared about money when she believed that he was only a navy pilot. Why should her feelings change because she now knew so much more about him?

Strange how heavy she felt suddenly, as if her heart was made of lead. She had to force herself to lift her head and meet his angry gaze, but pride demanded it. "You're right," she conceded. "I wasn't attracted to you until I found out about your land and titles, then I set out to hook you, so I can become Duchess of Norbourg and live in the castle forever."

It was so close to her fantasy, but for entirely different reasons, that her voice almost broke. She forced the last words out, "I thought a man who had dreamed up something as special as the *Pathfinder* project was someone I could care about after all, but it seems I was wrong."

She had startled him, she saw from the sudden narrowing of his eyes. No more than she had startled herself. She hadn't meant to confess what she knew, and it hurt to have him think his status mattered to her more than Ben himself did.

He prowled to the window and gazed out. Dusk

was falling over Eden Cove and lights had come on in some of the boats, creating little islands of radiance in the gathering dark. One of them went off inside her head. Meagan got up and went to Molly.

The child looked at her in alarm. "What's wrong, Mummy?"

She lifted Molly into her arms. "Nothing sweetheart, nothing at all. Mummy's finally come to her senses, that's all."

Snatching up the teddy bear, she carried Molly back to their room and began to pack.

Chapter Eight

Molly's small features contorted. "Don't want to go home. I like it here. I want to go in the sea."

The small cry tore at Meagan's heartstrings. But she knew she would have an uphill job to convince Shane that she had returned home willingly, so the sooner they went back, the better. It was the only way she could think of to protect Molly. "I'll take you paddling in the sea another time," she promised. "Right now, we have to leave. Won't it be fun being back home again?"

Molly shook her head. "Don't want to."

Meagan's eyes misted, and she had to force herself to keep packing. Molly wasn't the only one who wanted to stay. "That makes two of us, sweetheart, but some men are too stubborn to change." Especially men who expected modern women to behave like hothouse flowers. His late fiancée hadn't, and Meagan herself didn't. She was used to fending for herself, and his suggestion that money or a title mattered to her was insulting.

Her fingers curled around a tiny velvet dress she had made entirely by hand, the stitches so small they were practically invisible. Tears stung her eyes but she banished them by force of will. Ben didn't deserve her tears. "When you grow up, don't let any man tell you there are things you can't do because you're female," she told Molly. "You can be adventurous and have a career, and do anything they can do."

"I can do lots of things." To prove it, Molly piled her doll and a pillow from the bed into the suitcase.

Meagan retrieved the pillow. "We can't take things that belong here." Never mind that Ben had taken something precious to *her*—her heart. He didn't want it, and she wasn't going down that road again. Once was more than enough.

She gave a mighty sniff. "I won't stay with a man who doesn't know the difference between a gold digger and a woman who cares about him."

"Perhaps it's time somebody explained it to me."

The quiet comment from the doorway made her spin around. How much had Ben heard? Everything, she saw from the gleam in his gaze. She looked away, mortified. Now he knew how she felt, the last thing she had wanted him to know.

She crammed the remainder of Molly's clothes into

the suitcase, dashing her hand across her eyes to stem the threat of tears. She would not cry in front of him. After Kevan, she had vowed never again to let any man hurt her to that extent. There was no need to let Ben see how successfully he had managed it.

He took her hand and kissed the back of it. "Didn't you hear what I said?"

"Yes," she snapped, trying unsuccessfully to reclaim her hand.

Ben's grip tightened. "I mean it. I need you and Molly to show me how this relationship business works. I'm obviously not very good at it. First I try to wrap you in cotton wool, then I accuse you of angling for wealth and titles when it's obvious you're doing perfectly well without them."

The heat from his hand traveled all the way along her arm and through her body, pooling near her heart until she could hardly breathe. She took refuge in anger. "I'm glad you realize I'm not like that."

"I've realized a lot of things today. One of them is that I don't want you to leave."

She used her free hand to gesture around them. "There's no reason for us to stay. If my brother or his friends did plant that device, they know where we are by now."

"So you're going back so Shane will think you didn't want to leave in the first place?"

"Can you think of a better idea?"

"Taking you to the castle where you'll be safe."

Depended how you defined *safe,* she thought. She

had dreamed of Ben wanting her to stay, but not like this. Not out of some misguided sense of protectiveness. She could manage alone. She'd been doing it since Cousin Maude died. She would go on doing it long after Ben had forgotten she existed. She hated to think how little time that was likely to take. "You've made your feelings about me quite clear. I can cope."

"What if Shane doesn't buy the idea that you came with me under duress?"

She knew her brother too well. "He will because he wants to believe it."

Ben's hands balled into fists at his sides. "I can't believe you'd risk Molly's safety because of wounded pride. I've apologized for jumping to the wrong conclusion. What more can I do?"

Accept me just as I am, she thought futilely. "It's forgotten," she lied.

"Then prove it. Come back to the castle with me."

She wavered, trying to summon the will to argue with him, knowing it meant arguing with herself, as well.

He saw her hesitate. "You owe it to your child to let me protect you both."

The little girl lay on her stomach on the floor, small arm outstretched as she tried to retrieve a shoe from beneath the bed. Watching her, Meagan felt her resistance crumble. "Very well, but only until it's safe for us to return home."

"We'll leave first thing tomorrow." At the door, he turned. "Did you mean it when you told Molly you care about me?"

She felt her throat almost close. "I never lie to Molly."

He recrossed the room in two strides. "Yet you could walk away?"

"I don't know." She had intended to cross that bridge when she came to it—if she could.

"Then let me influence your decision." He kissed her, the heat of it swirling through her, turning her bones to jelly.

When he let her come up for air, she was shaking. "That isn't fair."

His heated gaze lingered on her face. "All's fair in love."

"This isn't love." At least not on his side, as far as she knew. Apprehension gripped her. Could his feelings for her amount to more than she suspected?

He grazed the side of her face with his knuckles, sending a shiver of pleasure through her. "It definitely isn't war."

Molly popped out from under the bed, holding a shoe triumphantly aloft. She regarded them suspiciously. "Are you and Mummy playing Sleeping Beauty?"

His arms still tight around her, Ben turned slightly. "Yes, Molly, but I'm the one finally waking up." His eyes were warm as he shifted his gaze back to Meagan. "The story could have a happy ending if the princess would marry me."

As marriage proposals went, this one took the cake, Meagan thought. It wasn't fair of Ben to include Molly. The child wasn't to know he didn't mean a word he said.

Molly's eyes shone. "You'll be a really truly princess, Mummy."

Ben slid a finger under her chin, lifting it. "Listen to your daughter, Meagan. You might not be a princess, but you would be my duchess."

The title meant nothing to her, but the thought of being Ben's wife made her heart drum a frantic tattoo. Could he possibly be serious about wanting to marry her? "I thought you didn't want to marry."

"I didn't want to get involved with anyone again, but this is another matter. We need one another. By helping me to escape, you've crossed the people who hold King Michael captive. That puts you and Molly in great danger. As my fiancée, you'd be under my personal protection from now on."

Given the way she felt about him, could she consider accepting his proposal, knowing he didn't return her feelings, and probably never would? For Molly's sake, she knew there could be only one answer. "Yes."

Molly gave a whoop of delight. "I'm telling Hannah."

Ben swept Molly into the embrace with them. "We have to tell my aunt, Queen Josephine, first. Until she gives us her blessing, it has to be our secret. Can you keep a secret?"

Molly made a heart-crossing gesture. "I won't even tell Mr. Snug."

"Good. Bears are such blabbermouths," Ben said straight-faced. He tightened his hold on Meagan. "For now, this is between the three of us."

Within the warmth of his embrace, Meagan wished she could shake off the cold hand of fear that clutched at her heart.

Ben must find her car very different from what he was used to, Meagan thought. She corrected the car's erratic steering so automatically that she didn't notice until Ben commented on it. "It's not luxurious but it does for Molly and me," she said.

He heard the quaver she couldn't keep out of her voice. "Are you all right? I should be driving."

When they'd set off from his house, she had refused his offer, assuring him she was fine. Now she wasn't so sure. "My child went missing so I thought she'd been kidnapped, someone bugged my car and there may be a traitor within the castle. Why wouldn't I be all right?"

Her emotions were also on a roller-coaster ride since she had agreed to marry him. The closer they got to the castle, the more convinced she was that she was out of her mind.

"Stop the car now," he insisted.

She responded to his tone of command reluctantly. She should have known he wouldn't treat her as an equal simply because she had accepted his proposal.

When she pulled up at the edge of the forest, he came around to the driver's side and helped her out of the car, although he had to fight her car's contrary locking system to do so. He glanced into the back seat where Molly slept peacefully, her teddy bear in her arms, unaware of the dread that clung to Meagan like a pall. Meagan knew she would do anything to protect her precious child, even marry Ben.

A truly noble intention, if Meagan hadn't wanted to marry him for her own sake, she thought.

When she stood up, he startled her by pulling her into his arms. It felt exactly right as she let him enfold her. She started to sniffle, hating herself for being so weak. He didn't seem to mind. "That's it, let it go."

Her tears flowed in earnest and he held her, murmuring words of comfort as if he really didn't mind that she was saturating the front of his shirt. He didn't seem to be in any hurry to release her. "I suppose you're used to this kind of thing," she gulped.

He shook his head. "It's been a while since a beautiful woman cried in my arms."

He wanted to make her feel better, she recognized, troubled by how well he was succeeding. "I meant this cloak-and-dagger business," she argued. "You are a military man."

He tilted her chin up and she saw that his face was grave. "I may have chosen a military career, but I prefer to find diplomatic solutions to problems whenever possible."

"And if you can't?"

"I wade in with the coffeepot, just as you did on my behalf."

Meagan's laughter was so musical and sweet that Ben felt his insides constrict in response. Since the king's disappearance, there hadn't been much laughter within the royal family, and Ben had missed it. The last few days had exacted a toll on him, too. He welcomed Meagan's warmth as a tonic he badly needed.

When the embrace changed from comforting to passionate, he wasn't sure, but suddenly his mouth sought hers with the certainty of a ballistic missile. He had seen the way they homed in on their target with unerring accuracy, and he felt the same directional pull now, the same primal need to seek out and conquer.

As his fingers threaded through her hair, he felt the ground shift under him. She exploded like a target, returning his fire with a volley of her own that left him dazed, breathless, hungry for more.

The battle images continued to hammer at him. He felt the adrenaline rush he usually experienced flying a Sea Harrier, as he played her mouth with all the sensitivity at his command. A slight pressure here, a tilt to the left there. He invaded her mouth and she bucked under his hands, but there was no withdrawal and no surrender.

Who was conquering whom? he wondered with what remained of his sanity. He'd bet she had never flown a Harrier, but she sensed exactly which of his buttons to press to make him explode with desire.

He shouldn't want this, he told himself. He wanted her, but it wasn't the same thing. He didn't want to feel so involved with a woman whose behavior reminded him so painfully of Marina's. He didn't want to love another woman who insisted on putting herself at risk the way his late fiancée had done. Yet Meagan was leading the formation and he couldn't make himself break off.

She did it for both of them, pulling out of the dive and coming in for a landing about a meter away from him, her eyes blazing residual fire at him. "What exactly was that?"

"Just a kiss."

Her breath came in heaving gulps. "That wasn't *just* a kiss. It was…"

"Open warfare?" he supplied, unable to stop himself from thinking in those terms.

Meagan nodded, speech eluding her for a moment. She couldn't condemn herself for letting him comfort her. After all that had happened she could even justify it. But she couldn't allow herself to be swept away every time he so much as touched her.

"I've agreed to marry you to protect Molly, but there it has to stop."

"It seems that Molly's father has a lot to answer for," he said, catching her unawares. "I will never let you down the way he did."

His fingers burned her arms through her thin shirt. Wildfire leapt from the points where he touched, raced along her nerves and exploded somewhere around her heart. How could a touch affect her so much? It didn't make sense. "You told me yourself you aren't promising me a real marriage. You don't believe in forever."

He released her, then turned back to the car. "Perhaps not, but I am promising there will be no other in my life but you."

Fine words, she thought, wishing with all her heart that she could rely on them.

Chapter Nine

The gulf between them had widened into a canyon by the time they reached the gates of Edenbourg Castle, she felt. An armed guard saluted crisply, operating the electronic controls to admit them to the walled citadel. If he found Ben's mode of transport unusual or thought it odd that he should have a strange woman and a little girl on board, the guard didn't show it by so much as a raised eyebrow.

Ben steered the car behind a screen of bushes, and all three of them got out. Then he walked back and made a telephone call from the guard's station. Within minutes a tall, steel-haired manservant joined them. Ben introduced him as James. The warmth she noticed between them suggested that James was a long-time family retainer. He fairly radiated trust and discretion. At Ben's instigation, James took her keys and drove her car away.

She felt as if a lifeline had been cut. "Where is he taking my car?"

"Out of sight," Ben said. "The same place I'm taking us. I'm keeping my return quiet until I've conferred with my aunt."

He led her through an almost-invisible door in a massive stone wall. The door closed behind them, and she found herself in a tunnel lit by a narrow window high above her head. She shivered slightly in the sudden coolness after the warmth of the sunshine outside. "I'd heard the castle was honeycombed with secret passages but I never thought I'd use one."

He picked Molly up, and took Meagan's hand. "This takes us directly to the queen's sitting room. I'll report to her before reappearing as Ben Lockhart."

"Won't your absence cause comment?"

"I had James put it about that I was laid up with a virus."

Meagan nodded, finding the passageways cold enough to give anybody a chill. She knew parts of the castle dated back to the tenth century, although it had changed its appearance many times over the years. The present head of state lived here now, and members of the royal family kept apartments in the vast grounds.

Could she ever feel at home in a place that boasted a history from the Middle Ages to the present? Meagan wondered. "This place is more like a community than a castle," she observed.

"That's exactly how it operates. Do you like the castle, Molly?"

The little girl in his arms nodded, her eyes sparkling with excitement. "Are you a real prince?"

"My mother is Princess Karenna of Wynborough, and my father is a captain in the navy. Will that do?" he asked.

Molly looked unimpressed. "Want to see the queen."

Ben gave Meagan a wry look. "Obviously the navy doesn't rate with a three-year-old. I hope she isn't too disappointed that Aunt Josephine doesn't wear a fairy-tale dress and crown."

Meagan felt uncertainty sweep through her. He may have proposed marriage to her, a commoner, but his aunt was still the Queen of Edenbourg. "I'm not dressed to meet the queen," she said, taking refuge in the most basic of female concerns.

"My aunt will be more interested in what we have to tell her than in how we look."

She might not share her brother's extreme views, but Meagan agreed with Shane that an accident of birth shouldn't decide an individual's worth any more than the make and model of their car or their mode of dress. Fortified by this thought, she straightened her spine as she marched beside Ben along the passage-way. Without him, she would have been lost in minutes. He guided them unerringly until he opened a door into a beautifully furnished salon.

After making another phone call, Ben told her that

Queen Josephine was meeting with Edward Stanbury who had taken on the king's responsibilities as soon as Nicholas had disappeared. Edward would continue in that capacity until the emergency was over.

To Ben it seemed strange to have his uncle's brother wearing the crown of Edenbourg. A little suspicious, too, since the entire drama had begun with Edward's return to the country with his American-born sons, Luke and Jake.

By saving Nicholas from the first kidnapping attempt, Jake had more or less exonerated himself. And unless Nicholas had somehow set up the attempt to make himself appear innocent, he was off the hook, too. But there was no certainty in any of it, and Ben felt frustrated by the lack of progress.

As soon as his aunt received word that Ben was back, she hurried to join them. In her fifties, the queen was reed-slender, her posture enviably upright. She had thick brown hair coiled into a chignon, and piercing green eyes. Although Ben knew she must be burning with impatience for news of her husband, she greeted Meagan and Molly cordially, and Ben warmly.

"King Michael is still alive," he said, knowing this was what she most wanted to hear.

Josephine inclined her head, only betraying by the momentary closing of her eyes, the relief that must be sweeping through her. "Is Michael well?" she asked Ben.

"I'm told he has suffered a slight stroke," he said, hearing her indrawn breath that, from anyone else, would have been a cry of dismay. "He's in the care of a doctor and is expected to recover. That's all I was able to learn," he concluded.

The queen's gaze went to Ben's fading bruises. "From the look of you, the price of what you did learn was quite high enough."

"It's nothing," he said dismissively. In truth he felt tired to the bone, but it had been worth it to bring some slight measure of relief for his aunt's suffering.

The queen frowned. "All the same, you should see the palace doctor."

"I told him the same thing on the way here, ma'am," Meagan contributed, frustrated that Ben wouldn't listen even to the queen. Ben's rough treatment while captured might have done more damage than he realized.

It hadn't prevented him from kissing her, she read in the look he gave her. At the thought, desire swamped her, hot and dizzying, forcing her to tear her gaze away from his face before she betrayed herself to the queen, or worse, to Ben himself.

She was afraid that the queen saw it anyway, and the corners of her mouth lifted. "Ben is not known for taking advice," she pointed out. "Perhaps you'll have better fortune with him."

"I wouldn't presume to try," Meagan said. Perversely she felt cheated that Ben hadn't introduced her to the queen as his fiancée, although she understood that he probably felt it was the wrong time. Would there ever be a right time? Maybe he was regretting having asked her to marry him.

Ben made a restless movement. "If you ladies have finished discussing me…"

Josephine's face betrayed traces of amusement. "Darling Ben, we haven't even begun." She leaned toward Meagan. "We shall continue this discussion at high tea this afternoon."

"What's high tea?" Molly chimed in. She had been remarkably good, too distracted by a bow-fronted cabinet filled with crystal animals to say much, Meagan decided.

"It's when one drinks tea and eats a full meal, and then delicious sweets," the queen explained. "Children usually have milk instead of tea."

Molly nodded. "I like milk and cake. But no 'cumber sandwiches."

"Then you shan't be made to eat them."

Molly regarded Josephine with suspicion. "If you're the queen, where's your crown?"

"Molly!"

Josephine comforted Meagan with a look, then smiled at the little girl. "It's kept in a special glass case, and only taken out on state occasions."

Meagan could feel her daughter burning to ask more questions, but squeezed her hand warningly. "Enough, Molly. The queen is very busy."

"Not too busy to see her favorite nephew, especially when he has risked so much for our sake," Josephine said with a fond look at Ben. "I'll send word to the doctor to expect you shortly." She pressed a discreet switch near her hand and a footman appeared within seconds. The queen gave instructions for Meagan and Molly to be given rooms near the apartment reserved for Ben when he was at the castle.

Meagan felt a surge of panic at the prospect of being separated from Ben in such a daunting environment, but he touched her hand in reassurance. The fleeting contact was enough to ignite flames of longing inside her. This would have to stop, she told herself sternly. She couldn't keep depending on him. She had stood on her own two feet since her late teens, and could go right on doing it.

"Thank you for your hospitality, ma'am, but might it not be better if Molly and I returned to my home?" she suggested.

Josephine glanced at Ben. Meagan didn't miss the decisive shake of his head. She felt like throttling him.

"Your home is where Ben was imprisoned?" the queen asked.

"Yes, but…"

"Then there is danger for you and your child if you return. I prefer that you remain here."

Ben had said the same thing. Meagan knew when she was outnumbered. She inclined her head in acquiescence. "Then we'll be glad to stay, ma'am, thank you."

"I'll see you again at tea," Ben told Meagan before she was escorted out.

"A charming woman with a sensible head on her shoulders. Pretty head at that," Josephine told him when they were alone. "She obviously has your well-being at heart."

"You may as well know, I've asked her to marry me," Ben admitted.

The queen gave him a surprised look. "You must care about her a great deal."

"She tended to me while I was a captive, and helped me to escape at considerable risk to herself."

"Those are hardly reasons for marriage."

"They're my reasons." His tone told her that he didn't want to discuss it further.

The corners of the queen's mouth twitched. "Then you have our blessing. And our deepest gratitude for what you risked for our sake."

"For all the good I did. We still don't know where King Michael is being held."

"But we know he is alive. For now, it must suffice. Now, off to the doctor with you."

Princess Isabel was in the salon when Ben arrived for high tea. She brought a message that the queen wouldn't join them after all. She had retired to her apartment, making Ben wonder if the shock of hearing about the king's stroke was catching up. He made a mental note to check with her lady-in-waiting later.

"Mother told me what happened to you. What did the doctor say?" Isabel demanded.

Ben helped himself to tea from a silver pot, adding two sugars and earning a disapproving tut-tut from his athletically inclined cousin. He defiantly added another, needing the energy boost. What with bruised ribs and rope burns on his wrists, he had known better days. "I'll live," he said shortly.

Isabel inspected him as if he was one of her prize horses. "I'll bet the other guy looks a lot worse."

Ben nodded. "They were unconscious when we left."

"We?"

Quickly he filled her in on Shane Moore's role in the kidnapping and Meagan's bravery.

Her eyes were full of questions, none of which he felt inclined to answer.

"Your Meagan sounds like quite a woman," she said.

"She isn't *my* Meagan. She's a grown woman with a three-year-old child."

"Who makes my dear cousin protest far too much."

"You're as bad as Aunt Josephine," he grumbled. "Surely you all have more pressing things to worry about than my love life."

He regretted his outburst when he saw a shadow cross Isabel's lovely features. "You're right, we do. When I heard you were back, I asked Adam Sinclair to join us. As the head of the security detail, he ought to hear what you and your...what you and Meagan have learned."

Ben nodded, more than willing to share any scrap of information with the other naval officer whom he both liked and respected. He was happy to leave the matchmaking to his aunt, but couldn't help thinking what an interesting couple Adam and his cousin made. The only two who didn't seem to realize it were Isabel and Adam themselves.

It was Meagan's fault that his thoughts kept heading in such dangerous directions, Ben decided. Over the last couple of years he had given far more attention to his work than to his romantic life. This was the first time in many moons that he had found himself thinking of love, and usually at the same time as he thought of Meagan. He still wasn't sure why he had proposed marriage to her. Telling himself it was for her protection didn't quite satisfy him as an explanation. Adam Sinclair's people could watch over her as well as Ben could. So what was going on here?

As if to prove his point, Meagan appeared at the salon door, hesitating on the threshold when she saw Princess Isabel with Ben. Was it the sight of his much-photographed royal cousin, or himself that brought Meagan up short? Ben wondered. She was having much the same effect on him, he found.

She had obviously allowed someone from the staff to provide her with a change of clothes. The effect was extraordinary, especially on his blood pressure. He felt it notching a few points higher as he looked at her.

She had looked pretty fantastic in the simple T-shirts she'd bought after they fled from her house. Now, in a softly draped teal-colored tunic and black leggings that fitted her shapely legs very nicely, she looked good enough to eat. She had done something to her hair, too. He had only seen it falling in a tumble of curls to her shoulders. Not that he had any complaints, but he liked this new style, fluffed out and caught behind her ears with a couple of combs. There seemed to be twice as much of it, and the curls practically invited a man to run his fingers through them.

"Come in, you must be Meagan," Isabel said warmly. "It seems that Ben has temporarily lost the power of speech. He was telling me how brave and selfless you are. And this must be Molly. Go and choose a cake for yourself," she urged the little girl.

Molly didn't need a second invitation. She skipped across the room to where dozens of small cakes, pastries and sandwiches were displayed on tiered silver servers. Choosing would take her some time, Meagan knew from experience. Molly was given such treats so rarely that she liked to savor them.

"I hope Ben didn't make me sound too heroic," Meagan insisted. "I was in the wrong place at the wrong time."

Isabel's forest-green eyes glinted. "Oh, he made your role perfectly clear."

When she didn't elaborate, Ben stepped forward. "Would you like some tea?"

Meagan hesitated. "This feels strange, given that the king is still a captive."

"Aunt Josephine wants life in the kingdom to go on as normally as possible," he said quietly, understanding Meagan's hesitation. He had taken some persuading himself before agreeing to participate in a ritual that seemed trivial, given what the king was going through. But as a military man, he also understood the value of routine when life was far from normal.

He fetched Meagan a cup of Earl Grey tea. "Isabel

and I were planning our next move." He didn't add that his love life had also been under discussion. No sense in giving Meagan the wrong idea. No sense telling Isabel that he and Meagan were engaged to be married, either. He could imagine what his cousin would make of that. She would find out when he was ready to make a public announcement, not before.

"The head of the security detail on the case is joining us shortly," Isabel added. "He'll want to talk to your brother."

Remembering her last sight of him slumped on the floor, Meagan shuddered. "Shane won't cooperate."

Ben saw her reaction. "You don't have to be involved anymore. The security people can handle things from here."

She shook her head. "I want to be. I know Shane better than anyone."

Ben would have vetoed the idea on the spot, aware of more than ordinary protectiveness influencing him. Meagan wasn't putting her life on the line if he could prevent it. He knew his attitude was out of date. Even in his own line of work, women handled just about every job. But he didn't care about them as much as he did Meagan. She had helped to save his life, he rationalized, not sure if it was the only reason for his feelings.

Isabel sensed his resistance, and stepped between them. "Meagan's right," she insisted. "It's her house. She has a right to be involved."

Ben's angry glance flashed to his cousin. Why did

every woman in his life want to be superwoman? "Shouldn't you let Adam and his team handle this?"

"I won't be treated like a child, Ben," Meagan said quietly and he heard the undercurrent of steel in her tone. "The queen has assigned a security guard to us and a nanny to Molly. She'll be safe here while I go with you. There's no way I intend to be left behind."

Anger knifed through him and something else. Desire such as he hadn't felt in a long, long time. He didn't want to feel either, but around Meagan, he didn't seem to have much choice. "Very well. But if you insist on going along, you'll follow my orders, understood?"

Chapter Ten

"You don't have to do this, Meagan. It's not too late to change your mind and wait outside while Adam and I go in," Ben told her.

"Adam and *Isabel* and I," came a resentful prompt from the back seat.

Along with Jake Stanbury, who had counted himself into the operation the moment he heard about it, and Adam's hand-picked security detail, they sat in a pair of blacked-out vans on the edge of the forest, out of view from Meagan's house.

Meagan squared her shoulders. This was her home and her brother. She was seeing it through. But Ben's concern warmed her. It had been a long time since anyone had cared so much about her. She had to remind herself that, to him, she was only a means to an end, the rescue of King Michael.

Ben would deny he was using her, of course. He might have convinced himself she meant something to him. But as long as he refused to let himself love again, theirs could be nothing more than a marriage of convenience. More than likely, it would end with the current crisis. The thought was more depressing than she knew it should be.

All the same, Ben's kisses promised a heaven Meagan yearned for with all her heart. For the first time she truly understood how it felt to be consumed by desire. Like the rest of the group, Ben was dressed all in black, his turtleneck sweater and pants making him look like a panther in human form, she thought. Desire for him gripped her like a fever she had to fight to shake off.

Adam Sinclair was supposed to lead the group, but Ben was the one the men deferred to instinctively, she had noticed. Alpha male, she found herself thinking. From what she had seen, Adam more than qualified for the title, so what did that make Ben? Was there such a man as alpha-plus?

"Ready?" he touched her arm, and she was proud of keeping her reaction down to a slight tremor. She nodded. Then he had to spoil the moment by saying, "Stay behind me as we approach the house."

Adam had briefed them beforehand. No heroics, he had said, looking straight at Meagan and Isabel. Meagan's job was to try to reason with her brother, get him to let them know the king's whereabouts, and the identity of the leader. But she didn't like Ben reminding her of what he imagined was her place.

The team's task was to arrest Shane and Dave, and return them to the castle for further questioning. All over in five minutes.

Best-laid plans, she thought. As soon as Adam identified himself and called to Shane to give himself up, shots were loosed at the group from inside the house. Meagan ducked instinctively, but stood her ground, sure that Shane wouldn't shoot her.

She gasped as Ben dragged her into a hedge. "Crazy woman, you're not bulletproof."

She struggled in his hold, then gasped as a searing pain shot up her leg from her left ankle. She had twisted her ankle on a tree root as she ducked Shane's first shots. She bit her lip, refusing to let Ben see that she was hurt. "Let me go. Shane will talk to me, I know he will."

Ben looked furious. "And he might also shoot you. Stay here. That's an order."

The pain in her ankle argued against defying him, but he didn't need to know that. She set her jaw into a mutinous line.

She saw Adam lead his team around the side of the cottage. By now, Meagan knew that Isabel and Jake should be in position at the back. On the way from the castle, Meagan had learned that the princess had served in naval intelligence, so she was well qualified for this mission. Adam had been her commanding officer before the king summoned her back to royal life. Given Isabel's background, Ben's objection to her involvement seemed illogical.

He didn't want her here either, Meagan recalled. He was a chauvinist who thought women needed mollycoddling, and he had to learn that she wouldn't put up with it for much longer.

Another shot rang out from the rear of the house, and Ben set himself to move. "I'm going in."

"Not without me." She struggled to her feet, biting her lip as pain radiated through her from her damaged ankle.

This time she couldn't conceal it from him. He ground out an oath and thrust her back into the shelter of the hedge. "You're not going anywhere. You can barely stand."

His attitude fired her anger. "A damaged ankle won't stop me from doing my part."

"But I will. You'll stay here voluntarily, or I'll handcuff you to this tree for your own good. Your choice."

She knew he carried handcuffs as part of the arsenal he'd gathered for the mission, and didn't doubt that he meant what he said. She subsided, fuming. "I'll stay here."

He claimed her mouth in a lightning kiss that tore through her like flame, before he zigzagged across the front courtyard. She saw him shoulder-roll to the door, then spring to his feet and break the door down with a well-aimed kick. He flung himself inside.

Shouts and shots assaulted her ears, then silence.

Was Ben all right? Every fiber of her being refused

to accept that that kiss could be his last earthly experience. She knew he had only kissed her as an alternative to handcuffing her, to ensure she followed his orders, but it didn't change the effect on her.

Unable to stay still a moment longer, she made herself count to twenty then limped around the perimeter of the courtyard until she could peer inside. Her heart slammed against her chest as she saw black-clad male legs sprawled in a doorway.

"Great oceans, not Ben. Please, not Ben." On legs that felt mired in molasses she forced herself to take a painful step inside, clinging to the wall to take the weight off her protesting ankle.

Before she had taken more than two steps, she was caught in strong arms and carried out into the courtyard. She fought and clawed. She had to see, to know. If Ben *was* dead, she knew her world would never be the same again.

The arms held her, refusing to yield. "It's all right, everything's all right."

The world spun around her. "Ben, you're not dead."

"Obviously not."

She struggled to free herself, to see. "Then who…"

His hold tightened. "You're not to go in there. It's Shane."

The next day, lying on a chaise in the vast apartment the queen had allocated for her use, Meagan felt more alone than ever. In truth she *was* alone. Her brother, her last surviving relative, apart from Molly, was dead, killed by Luke Stanbury when he had seen Shane take aim at Princess Isabel. Unlike his brother, Jake, who Ben had said was no longer under suspicion, Luke hadn't been included in the original team. Ben had told Meagan that Luke had invited himself along after his father told him what was planned. For Isabel's sake, it was as well he had, Meagan thought.

When they returned to the castle, Edward had hailed his son as a hero for saving the princess's life. It was the first time Meagan had seen Edward, and she was alarmed at how frail he looked, the strain of his sudden elevation to the throne telling on him.

She noted that Edward was the only one lauding his son's bravery. Meagan had heard Isabel and Adam pondering aloud whether Luke's act was as heroic as it seemed, or if he had invited himself along in order to silence a fellow conspirator. From Ben, Meagan knew that rumors were flying around the castle over the king's disappearance. It was hard to credit that the informant within the castle could be any of the royal family she had met so far. They seemed united in their determination to see King Michael safely restored to the throne.

She knew beyond a doubt that Ben was incapable of treachery. He had endangered himself by impersonating Prince Nicholas, and had put his life on the line again to try to capture Shane and his partner. Dave had also died in the skirmish. Ben had told her that one of the security men had killed him when the giant turned a gun on the team.

She remembered how Ben had helped her back to her suite last night after the doctor had checked her X rays and instructed her to rest her ankle.

Ben had lingered, sensing that she needed the company, although she hadn't known how to answer when he asked, "Are you all right?"

She had answered truthfully. "I don't know."

"It's too bad we didn't get a chance to question Shane," Ben had said, "but Luke assured us there was nothing else he could do." He rammed a fist into his palm. "We've reached a dead-end."

"Perhaps not." She had limped to a writing desk under the window and retrieved a sheet of paper she'd started working on before the raid. She still didn't know why she'd felt the need to do it, but now she was glad she had. "I've made you a list of as many of Shane's friends and contacts as I can remember. One of them might provide a new lead."

Ben accepted the paper, frowning. "Why didn't you think of this sooner?"

She looked down. "I thought you'd get the information from Shane himself."

"And you feared what he could do to Molly if he knew you'd informed on him," Ben guessed. "You're safe from him now."

"But not from his friends."

Ben's hand had covered hers. "To get to you, they'll have to go through me first. We'll give this list to Isabel. She and Adam Sinclair will put it to good use."

The touch of his hand sent tremors radiating

through her. Telling herself she was only feeling the aftereffects of the raid didn't entirely satisfy her.

By the time Meagan had been seen by the doctor, one of the royal attendants had bathed and fed Molly, which was just as well because Meagan had no idea how she would have managed it. For her child's sake, she contained her feelings while she read Molly a bedtime story and listened to the child's account of her day. Molly had been alarmed at the sight of the bandage on Meagan's ankle, until Ben had spun the child a convincing tale about her mummy catching her foot in a rabbit hole in the garden. Now Molly couldn't wait to see the rabbit.

Meagan felt a wan smile tug at her mouth. Her daughter hadn't stopped talking about the wonders of the castle, from the pretty flower gardens to the swing she'd been allowed to play on, and the swans Uncle Ben had promised to let her feed.

So it was Uncle Ben already. "Did he say you could call him that?" she had asked Molly after Ben had said good-night to the little girl.

The child's head had bobbed. "When we feed the baby swans, he's says I can name one. I'm calling him Strawbie."

"If it's a girl swan, shouldn't she be Raggedy-May?"

Molly had giggled. "Uncle Ben said that, too. He says lots of things like you do." Sitting up in bed, she had adopted a disturbingly familiar posture as she recited, "Don't touch that. Hold on to the railing on the stairs. Wash your hands." She'd taken a deep breath. "Is he a daddy?"

"Not at the moment," Meagan had said carefully. If she married him, he would be Molly's daddy. Meagan thrust the thought aside. She had agreed to marry Ben to ensure Molly's safety. With Shane gone, the danger had lessened, and with it Meagan's certainty that she was doing the right thing.

Molly had allowed herself to be tucked into bed. She had drifted off to sleep halfway through the story, leaving Meagan to deal with her troubled thoughts.

Now Molly was with Ben, feeding bread to the swans at the lake. Meagan would have liked to join them. Being left alone gave her too much time to think.

Shane had died last night, yet her first thought had been relief that it wasn't Ben. What kind of person did that make her? Shane had chosen his course freely knowing where it might lead, she told herself. Now she had to choose her own.

By the time Ben brought Molly back, Meagan's mind was made up. She and Molly would leave the castle as soon as Meagan could arrange it. Last night had shown her how deeply she had come to care for Ben. She couldn't contemplate marrying him, knowing he didn't feel the same.

"Swan babies have stripes," Molly announced, sounding impressed. "I wanted to hold one, but Uncle Ben said their mummy would get cross."

Meagan avoided meeting Ben's gaze. "I'm sure she would. Are you hungry?"

"The cook has lunch ready for her," Ben said. He signaled for the attendant. She curtsied to Meagan although she'd been told that it wasn't expected, and led Molly away by the hand.

"I've decided it's time for Molly and me to leave," Meagan said as matter-of-factly as she could.

"The doctor advised you to rest."

"I can rest at home."

"You can't want to return to that house?"

She wasn't looking forward to it, afraid she would imagine Shane's body on the floor whenever she passed that spot. But Isabel had assured her that Adam's people would erase all traces of the raid. "We can't stay here indefinitely."

"As my fiancée, you can stay as long as you choose. The queen will be disappointed, of course. She is expecting a wedding."

What about Ben himself? Meagan wondered. His cold, distant tone almost broke her heart. She waited for him to say he wanted her to stay, but it didn't happen.

"Even if you hadn't been injured in the service of the king, it isn't safe for you to return until the rest of the conspirators are caught. They could blame you for letting 'Prince Nicholas' escape, as well as for the loss of their comrades," Ben reasoned.

She lowered her lashes over troubled eyes. "They'd be right. Some of the responsibility is mine."

"Not as much as you're trying to take. Can't you let go and let me take care of you?"

She felt her eyes mist, wanting to give in so much

she could taste it. She had taken care of herself and her child for so long that she felt bone-weary. Some of the effect came from Shane's death and her injury, she knew, but the rest was cumulative, maybe going all the way back to when her secure world was torn asunder after her parents had drowned. She'd never really felt safe since then. Now old wounds she'd thought were long healed threatened to open up.

If she gave in to Ben now, she might never summon the strength to shoulder her burdens again. With no one else to turn to, how could she take the risk? "I can't," she said with a decisive shake of her head.

"Because you're afraid it will be too hard to start again afterward?" he said.

Tears welled up but she blinked them away angrily. "Of course not."

"You're not the only one who has had to pick themselves up and go on after losing someone you cared about."

"Mike Stafford told me about your fiancée."

Ben's bladed hand slashed the air. "Did he also tell you that her death was my fault?"

"Apparently you believe so. Mike doesn't agree."

"Mike didn't make the decision that got her killed. Marina was a pilot in my squadron, daughter of an admiral who admitted he would have preferred a son. She wanted to prove she could do anything a man could do. When I dropped her from a dangerous mission because she wasn't ready, she changed places with another pilot. An inquiry established that she'd misjudged her distance from the ground and lost control. She could have bailed out, but she waited till her navigator got out. In the end, she waited too long. She died three days before our wedding date."

"You can't blame yourself for her recklessness. We all have to face the consequences of our actions. Marina did. Shane did. I'm not immune."

"You think I'm wrong to want to protect you from harm?"

"Protect, but not smother."

"Yesterday you came within a hairbreadth of getting yourself killed."

"But I survived. I need breathing space, Ben, everyone does." She also needed his love, but nothing would come of saying so.

"At least stay until your ankle improves. After that, if you still want to leave, I won't try to stop you."

He hadn't asked her to stay for his sake, she noticed. Maybe she was right, and he *was* regretting his proposal. "Very well, I'll stay for now. But what about your injuries? You didn't exactly get off unscathed."

She had heard the doctor warn Ben that he had done more damage to his half-healed ribs. It must have happened when he broke into the house, she thought. He had shrugged off the doctor's concern, but the whiteness around his eyes and the care with which he moved wasn't lost on her. He was suffering too, but refused to give in to it.

That made two of them, she thought. By now she

knew better than to offer him sympathy he didn't welcome. "How are the others?" she asked instead.

"Isabel and Adam have their heads together planning strategy," he informed her. "My cousin should have been born to a warrior tribe instead of a royal family."

Meagan nodded. "She seems to thrive on action."

He grimaced. "She's never forgiven me for advising the king to bring her home from the navy when she wanted to extend her tour of duty."

"*You* advised him? Ben, how could you?"

"She's a princess, her place is here."

"You refuse to live here and be hidebound by protocol."

"It's different for Isabel."

Meagan felt her blood heat. "Because she's a woman? Or because you don't want to lose another woman the way you lost your fiancée?"

"What does it matter?"

"It matters because it's affecting how you treat women now." How he treated *her* now, Meagan acknowledged. That was really at the heart of her anger. "This may be a tenth-century castle, but the people living in it belong to this century and it's time you accepted it."

He loomed over her, his eyes blazing. "Have you quite finished?"

Would she ever be entirely finished with him? she wondered. In a short time he had made a devastating impact on her peace of mind. She tried to blame it on the unusual situation. They had been thrown together

in a crisis and it was bound to create an artificial closeness. It wasn't real, she assured herself.

Her response had nothing to do with his impact on
her as a woman. Was *that* why she resisted his
concern? Because she didn't want to feel so infuriat-
ingly female around him? No way was she admitting
that, even to herself. "It's enough for now," she said in
a betrayingly husky voice.

He heard it, too. "I should hope so. I came to check
on you, not to start an argument."

"It seems to be all we are able to start." And a good
thing, too, she thought unconvincingly. She wasn't about
to surrender control of her life to anyone, least of all a
man who thought a woman's place was in his castle.

"It does, doesn't it?" He dropped to the chaise, carefully avoiding contact with her bandaged ankle, and took
her hands. "When we're together, I find myself wanting
to do one of two things. The first is argue with you."

With her hands caught in his, she could hardly
breathe. "And the second?"

"This." He slid his hands around her shoulders,
gathering her against the hard wall of his chest. She
gasped as his lips touched her hair, then her brow, then
skimmed the side of her face. She felt the erratic
rhythm of his heart against her own. When his mouth
reached hers, the familiarity of his kiss sent shock
waves through her. Warm, demanding, giving sensations she was coming to know too well, want too much.
Yet she couldn't stop herself from returning his kiss.

She wasn't an innocent, but Ben made her feel like one. Every erotic touch felt new and vibrant, every skim of his mouth over hers like a promise of something she had yearned for without knowing it.

She wanted to give him everything of herself she had to give. It would be a mistake, but she couldn't keep the desire out of her responses. She wore only a light robe over a silky nightgown, and his hands slid under it, over the soft skin of her shoulders, kneading, warming, exciting. When he reached the swell of her breast, she dragged in lungfuls of air and still felt oxygen-starved. She dropped her head back, panting with the need for more air.

She struggled for control, but he took it away with every stroke of his sensitive fingertips over her heated skin. Pleasure warred with pain, desire with common sense. Pleasure and desire grew, until she was helpless in his arms. She shivered as he brought her to the brink of ecstasy, only to retreat again, prolonging the dizzying pleasure until she could hardly bear it.

Surrender. The word flamed in her mind, so insistently that the only possible answer was, "yes." It hovered on her lips, clamoring to be said, to be heard. She wanted Ben's possession more than she had ever wanted anything, so why fight it so strongly?

He sensed her resistance and lifted his head from her breast, his glazed eyes clearing slightly. "Am I hurting you?"

He was about to, she sensed. And she was as close to allowing it as she had ever been. "No," she said, since it was the only word she could force past lips swollen with desire.

He looked confused then angry. "Just…no? You can't deny that you want me as much as I want you."

She lowered her lashes over misting eyes. He must see his effect on her. Especially now, when she was about to throw away a gift she knew might never come again. The thought almost broke her, but she lifted her head. "I thought I did, but I was wrong. I can't marry you, Ben."

"Because?"

"Must I give a reason?"

With furious moves, he tugged her nightgown and robe back into place and hurled himself away from her. "Yes, you do. If you'd turned me down when I first asked you, it would have made sense. I would have concluded you weren't interested. But that's not true, is it?"

She couldn't meet his angry gaze. "You know it isn't."

"So you want me, and I want you. We're both free agents." His gaze suddenly intensified, fixing her until she felt like a rabbit in a hunter's spotlight. "Aren't we?"

He began to pace, bracing his damaged ribs with an arm across his chest. "After all that's happened, I can't believe you're still loyal to Molly's father." Knowing she'd added to his pain, Meagan felt brutal, but dared not retract. "That's it, isn't it?" he said in the manner of thinking aloud. "Is he one of the conspirators? Great oceans, is all this part of some devious plan?"

He had leapt way ahead of her, and her puzzlement was genuine. "What are you talking about? I've given you a list of Shane's contacts."

"If the names are genuine. Are you a plant, Meagan?"

"A plant? I don't understand."

"Is this whole exercise a scheme to get you inside the castle as your lover's agent?" He almost spat the word out. "What are you supposed to do on the inside? Make it easy for whoever wants the throne to get it? Tell me, Meagan."

He was shaking her, his fingers digging into her shoulders, and she felt hot tears start, but they were angry tears prompted by his lack of faith in her. In refusing to marry him, she had tried to protect herself. She had never dreamed he would decide that she was involved in some grand conspiracy. "You're hurting me," she said.

He released her, looking shocked. "I didn't mean to. What's come over me? You drive me to do things I'd never do ordinarily. I'd better go."

He looked pained as he stood up. "Don't go like this," she implored, feeling as if she must also be white to the bone.

He shook his head. "Around you, I'm not rational anymore. We'll talk tomorrow."

At least he had given her that much, she thought as the great carved door slammed behind him, the sound reverberating through her like a thunderclap. It wasn't what she yearned for, but she had forfeited her right to more, and the awareness made the pain in her ankle seem trivial by comparison.

She had never dreamed that he would misread her reluctance to marry him as loyalty to Molly's father. Now he thought she loved a man who was behind the abduction of the king and Ben himself. She ached to convince him he was wrong about her, but perhaps it was better to let him think what he liked. This way she could keep her emotional distance for her own self-preservation.

She had a feeling it would be easier said than done.

Chapter Eleven

A mother's instinct made Meagan's head lift from the historical novel she had taken from a well-stocked bookcase in the sitting room that opened off her bedroom. Molly was supposed to be asleep in the next room. The child couldn't possibly have called to her through the apartment's massively thick walls, but Meagan sensed that Molly needed her.

The little girl was standing up on the bed, her tiny form dwarfed by the antique furniture. At the sight of her mother, she rubbed her eyes and gave a tremulous smile. Smiling back, Meagan moved toward her, favoring her injured ankle, although it was much improved after her day of rest. "Bad dream?"

Molly nodded. "I called and called, but you didn't come."

Meagan enveloped the child in a hug. One thing she could say for the present-day royal family, they believed in central heating. The apartment was cosy, and Molly felt warm to her touch, although thankfully not feverish. "It was only a dream. I'm here now. Go back to sleep."

"I'm not sleepy."

Meagan settled the child on her lap, and stroked her fine hair. "Can't you pretend to be sleepy? You could be Sleeping Beauty."

Molly giggled. "I'm too little. You be Sleeping Beauty. Then Uncle Ben can kiss you awake."

Robbed of breath for a moment, Meagan wrestled herself under control. It was only a child's fantasy, the last thing Ben would be interested in. The last thing *she* should want. "I'm pretty sure Sleeping Beauty didn't have a bandage on her ankle," she said.

Molly climbed off her lap, planted a wet kiss in her palm, then patted it on to the bandage, making Meagan smile. "Poor Mummy. Kiss it better."

"That's much better, sweetheart," Meagan assured her. She put her weight on the ankle. Apart from a slight twinge, she stood easily. "See what a kiss can do?" If you didn't count the emotional havoc it caused when it came from a man she had no business kissing.

Molly took her hands. "Lie down, Mummy. Be Sleeping Beauty."

Knowing better than to prolong the scene by resisting, Meagan stretched out on Molly's bed. "Like this?"

Molly fussed around her, arranging her nightgown

and robe so they draped over the edge of the bed. She put a small hand over Meagan's eyes. "Now be asleep."

Meagan obediently closed her eyes, then opened one to peek at her child. "Since we don't have a prince handy, Mr. Snug had better kiss me awake."

"Oh, I think we can do better than that."

Meagan's eyes flew open to find Ben leaning over her, the last person she had expected to see tonight. He had evidently been taking a dip in the heated indoor pool he had shown her soon after they arrived, because his midnight-blue tracksuit was studded with damp patches, and a towel was slung around his neck. His face glowed with exertion.

She was afraid her color mirrored his, without the excuse of the exercise. "What are you doing here?" she asked.

"I thought a swim would help me to sleep. On my way back to my apartment, I saw Molly's door standing open. I heard voices so I looked in to make sure she was all right, in time to hear that you're short of a prince."

Tension gripped her. "You're a duke, not a prince. Just as well, because princes don't wear tracksuits."

"This one does. What do you think, Molly? Do I look royal enough?"

She giggled again. "No. But you can kiss my mummy."

His eyebrows lifted. "What if she doesn't want me to?"

"She has to, so she can wake up and marry you."

This had gone far enough. Meagan tried to scramble

to her feet, but Ben sat down on the side of the bed.
With the edge of her robe trapped under him, she
wasn't going anywhere.

It was only a game, she told herself. The sooner she
let him, in Molly's words, kiss her awake, the sooner the
little girl would go back to sleep. Then Meagan could
bid Ben good-night and return to her own room, alone.

Tension gripped her as Ben turned to Molly. "You'd
better tell me what to do."

"I don't know. I'm only three."

Ben leaned closer. "Perhaps the prince should take
Sleeping Beauty in his arms, like this."

Molly nodded, her expression pleased. Meagan
tried not to react as he slid an arm under her shoulders
and lifted her so she was cradled against him. He felt
hot and hard, the tracksuit barely disguising his taut
muscles. His dark hair was slick with water, but he still
managed to look disturbingly royal.

She closed her eyes, partly to please Molly, but also
because being so close to him was scrambling
Meagan's thought processes. It only served to concentrate her sensory awareness of him, sending her
pulse rate into overdrive. He smelled of shower soap
and masculinity. Through the silky robe his touch felt
electrifying. If this didn't end soon, she didn't know
what she was going to do.

She felt Molly scramble onto the bed beside her,
where she curled against the pillow with a sigh of satisfaction. "Good," she pronounced, sounding sleepy.
"Now you can wake Mummy up."

Ben's soft sigh whispered over Meagan's heated skin. "It seems a shame. She looks beautiful just as she is."

He was only saying it to please the little girl, Meagan told herself, trying unsuccessfully to subdue the feelings tearing through her like brushfire.

She felt sure she wasn't anybody's idea of a princess, although she would never have known it from the look she saw on Ben's face when she peeked at him through a fringe of lashes. He looked…transfixed, she thought, and found herself curiously unwilling to examine what it might mean.

Molly yawned hugely. "Mummy looks like a princess."

"Yes," Ben responded softly, his voice thickening. "Just like a princess."

His hands smoothed her hair away from her face as she had done for Molly a few moments before. But there any similarity ended. His touch spoke of very grown-up needs and desires.

It *wasn't* all on her side, she thought in wonder. She felt the strength of his desire in the way his fingers traced her features, lingering over her mouth before skimming along the line of her jaw.

Such a light touch. So innocent. But there was fire in his fingers, transmitted through her nerves like the lighting of a fuse.

Ben had imagined Meagan like this. No, not precisely like this. Not playing a game to please a child, although that, too, gave rise to dreams he knew he had no business indulging. It was all too easy to imagine Meagan as his wife, and Molly as their child as they shared a moment of family closeness together.

The thought led him to imagine himself alone with Meagan, when he could drink his fill of her, man to woman.

His hunger was reflected in the fast beating of his heart, and the fire inside him that threatened to turn into an inferno at any second. Each touch of his fingers to the curve of her lips made him want to taste all of her. He yearned to explore her secrets while giving her all that he was capable of giving.

He sensed that she would have as much to give as he would. Like him, she wasn't content to remain on the surface of any experience.

When they had first arrived, he had shown her around this wing of the castle. She had been as excited as her child. Molly's delight had been infectious as she touched every statue with curious fingers. Meagan had concealed her fascination better, but not from him. He had read the sparkle in her eyes and the bloom on her cheeks, and felt as if he was seeing the wonders of the castle for the first time himself.

Making love to her would be like the first time, too, he sensed. He couldn't help it. He lowered his mouth to hers and tasted.

A mistake. As soon as his lips met hers, desire threatened to swamp his rigid self-control. It took everything he had not to deepen the kiss, knowing where it must lead. Where it couldn't lead as long as she stubbornly refused to let him protect her.

The morsel he permitted himself was dangerous enough. It filled his head with thoughts of tearing aside her silk robe and gown, and taking her without ceremony. It would be dangerous and exhilarating, like riding out a force-ten gale at sea. Then, first passions sated, he would take the time to pleasure her with all the finesse at his command.

Lying in his arms she looked almost more beautiful than he could bear. More delicious than any food he had ever tasted. She didn't have to do anything to make him want her so much it was akin to pain.

His desire found its way into his kiss, so that when he ended it and her eyes flew open, he saw astonishment in her gaze. And something else. Recognition, he decided. She knew what he wanted, and her eyes said yes. He had to struggle to keep in mind that she still loved another man.

He saw the moment when she came back to reality. Her gaze became shuttered, and she plucked at his clothes as if she couldn't quite bring herself to push him away although she knew it was what she should do.

He made it simple for them both by easing her back against the pillow and standing up. He looked at the child curled up like a kitten, her breathing quiet and even. Mother and daughter looked so heart-stoppingly beautiful that an ache of longing fisted inside him, as powerful as it was unexpected. "It worked. Molly fell asleep."

Meagan turned her head, her gaze softening as she

looked at the sleeping child. It hardened when she looked back at him. "But you didn't stop."

The accusation in Meagan's tone was justified. He had seen the little girl drift off to sleep, unable to fight exhaustion any longer. He could have ended the kiss then but he hadn't. "I didn't want to," he admitted frankly.

"Why not?"

Slowly he ran a hand down the side of her face, and felt her shiver of response. "Do you need to ask?"

"I suppose not." She let her lashes close for a second, then opened them to look squarely at him, her expression accepting her part in what had just happened, whatever it was. She wasn't sure what to call it. Not love. Never love. Passion? Most definitely that, and more. It felt like a wholesale attack on every defense she possessed. "This has to stop," she insisted.

A flash of anger lit his expression before he masked it. "Because of your misplaced loyalty to Molly's father?"

She let her gaze answer, unable to find the strength to lie to him outright. He looked so cold that Meagan wished she had told him the truth about Kevan from the beginning, instead of hiding behind a man who had vanished from her life long before.

So why not be honest with Ben? Self-protection, she acknowledged. She had survived one man's deception, and built a life for herself and Molly. She didn't plan on leaving herself open to any man's blandishments again.

Until Ben.

Nothing in her careful planning had anticipated

him. With the lightest caress he made her want more than was sensible or attainable. As long as he thought she was in love with another of the conspirators, she might have some defense against him.

She should have been relieved when he bid her a terse good-night and strode out of Molly's room, but instead she felt empty and alone. Slowly she got up, covered the sleeping child and turned on the night-light, telling herself she had done the right thing, the only thing.

When she quietly walked between her suite and Molly's, she found him waiting in her sitting room. Still angry she saw, from the way he paced up and down in front of the unlit fireplace. Still impossibly handsome and compelling. Still a danger to her peace of mind.

"How is the ankle?" he asked, noticing her slight limp as she came in.

"Almost better. The doctor said I'll be able to use it normally after another night's rest." She wished she could say as much for her peace of mind.

"Is there something else?" she asked as coolly as she could, although it wasn't reflected in her inner temperature. "I'm tired, and I want to go to bed."

"We could, you know."

The internal heat banked higher. "What?"

"We could go to bed together. I know you have the crazy notion that you owe your loyalty to your child's father, but you said he's married. I gather he doesn't plan on leaving his wife for you, so why not pay him back in kind?"

"How does sleeping with you do that?" she demanded. Saying it out loud clogged her throat with desires she didn't want to feel.

"It gives you the chance to get even with him."

Just desserts, Meagan thought, annoyed with herself for the quick flash of anger. She had let Ben think she still cared about Molly's father, leading Ben to conclude that she'd welcome his suggestion. "What does it give you?"

"You."

The one word was almost her undoing. "Why do you want me when you can have any woman in the kingdom?"

"I don't want any woman in the kingdom."

And he only wanted her because he couldn't have her. If she told him there was no one else, would he still feel the same way? The admission hovered on her tongue, held back only by the fear that honesty would betray the depth of her love for him.

Then what would happen? He didn't want a lasting relationship. He had only proposed marriage to protect her and Molly. "We can't always have what we want," she said, speaking for herself.

"What do *you* want, Meagan?"

His question caught her off guard. "I have my daughter, my home, work I enjoy. They're enough for me."

His pacing brought him close to her, and he rested his hands on her shoulders, his gaze penetrating. "Are you sure? I notice there's no mention of love."

His nearness threatened to undermine what little resistance she had left. "I thought I was in love once. Look where it got me."

He started to knead her shoulders, reading the tension in them and dispelling it, only to trigger new kinds deep inside her that no amount of massaging would cure. She felt molten, unable to summon the strength to move away. "It got both of us this far," he said, his tone husky.

She shook her head, her hair pooling around her shoulders. "There is no us, Ben. If it wasn't for King Michael being abducted, we would never have met."

"But we did meet, and we both felt the pull from the beginning."

It wasn't a question. He knew she couldn't deny it.

"The point is, what are we going to do about it?"

Slight panic gripped her. "Why must we do anything? It's easier for a man. You're made to act on your passions, then move on. It's different for a woman."

His hold tightened. If he wasn't careful, she would have the marks of his fingers on her shoulders tomorrow, she thought. Branded, the way he would do to her soul if she wasn't careful.

"You seem sure I would move on," he said.

"It's what men do."

"It's not what I do."

Finding the strength at last, she tore herself out of his grasp. "Listen to yourself. You're the son of a princess. You may have chosen an ordinary life, but that's what it is, a choice. All you have to do is say the word to belong here again. I don't have that luxury. I don't belong here and I never will." Let him think she feared being out of place in the castle, instead of in his heart.

She clenched her hands. "Say we do give in to what we feel. Tonight it would be wonderful, I don't doubt. But tomorrow, what would I have then?" Not even her self-respect, she knew.

"I've already asked you stay."

"As what? You won't grant me—or any woman— equal status in your life."

"I regard you as my equal," he said in measured tones.

She could hardly speak, she was so angry. He regarded no female as equal. "I suppose next, you'll tell me you want our marriage to be real?"

"Not yet. As long as the country is in crisis, all I can offer you is an engagement, and the protection of being known as my fiancée."

"And you'll marry me as soon as the crisis is over," she supplied. "Surely you don't expect me to fall for a line like that?"

He looked frustrated. "How did we get into this? It isn't a line, it's the truth."

She splayed her hands, relieved to see they shook only a little. She had never wanted to lash out at a man as much as she wanted to at Ben at this moment. Couldn't he hear himself? "I believe you want to make love to me," she put in before he could interrupt. Dear heaven, she wanted it almost more than she could bear, but she made herself face reality. "You may believe you'll marry me as soon as the king is safely returned to the throne. But after he's found, something else will come up and you'll have to put our marriage off for a few more days or months. Or years," she added tiredly.

"Have you always been so cynical toward men?"

"Not all men." Only those who got under her defenses and made her want them, she thought. And not them, him. Until Ben came into her life, she had never felt such a powerful yearning for any man. If Molly's father hadn't come to her in despair, pretending to need her, she would never have given in to him. It hadn't happened again with him or anyone else.

She hadn't wanted it to, she recognized. Until now.

Ben raked long fingers through his hair, leaving trails in the damp strands. "Then I must be the problem. Do you dislike me so much?"

"Not dislike." Never that. "*Distrust* is probably a better word." Distrust of herself as much as of him, she recognized. The strain of these last moments proved beyond a doubt that she couldn't go on seeing him in any capacity, knowing all the love was on her side.

It was simple for him, she thought. To him, sex and love were separate issues, instead of being hopelessly connected the way they were for her. He had shown how little she could trust his talk of marriage. She should be thankful she hadn't allowed him to do more than kiss her.

Instead she felt more confused than ever. Falling in love with Ben was the biggest mistake of her life. She understood why it had happened. He was dependable, principled. Two of the qualities she found most attractive in a man. Yet as long as he didn't love her, they had nothing. She had thought she could marry him on his terms, but she couldn't.

"I told the queen I'd asked you to marry me," he said flatly. "She gave us her blessing."

"Did you tell her why you proposed to me?"

"I didn't have to. She understands the risk you took by deciding to help us."

Marrying for reasons other than love was probably normal within the royal family, Meagan thought. Evidently Queen Josephine hadn't found Ben's proposal remarkable. Perhaps the royal women accepted having their men run their lives for them as the price they paid for their privileged existence.

Then Meagan thought of Princess Isabel's determination to live her life her way. Things could be different. But Ben refused to accept his cousin's choice. What chance did Meagan have of changing his attitude toward women?

"The danger to you and Molly still exists," he continued grimly. "Adam is no closer to identifying the traitor within the castle."

"Are you sure Shane wasn't just talking big? If the traitor is one of the Stanbury family, wouldn't they have known that it wasn't the real Prince Nicholas they were abducting?"

He shook his head. "Only Prince Nicholas, my aunt and I knew that I was taking his place. Nicholas could have gone along with the scheme to make himself look innocent, but it seems unlikely, although it can't be ruled out completely. No one who has seen what my aunt has suffered since King Michael was abducted could think she has anything to do with the conspiracy."

"And you would hardly arrange to have yourself drugged, kidnapped and beaten," she said, hating that it had happened under her roof. "That still leaves a lot of suspects."

"Who have good reason to want you out of the way," he reminded her. "Tomorrow I shall make our engagement public to forewarn the conspirators that you're under my protection."

Panic coiled through her. She wasn't ready for this. As long as he didn't love her, she never would be ready. But his jaw was set, suggesting that he wouldn't take no for an answer. "I'll agree on one condition," she said.

"Name it."

"That you release me from the arrangement as soon as the crisis is over."

His look became coldly assessing. "If it's what you want."

"I do."

The two words were bitterly ironic, since she knew she'd never say them to Ben in the traditional way. Perhaps she'd never get to say them at all, for he was the only man she could imagine making wedding vows to, and while he might say them, she knew he didn't believe in them.

Chapter Twelve

Ben came into the antechamber to find Meagan bowed over a piece of fabric. Unreasoning anger swept over him. By proposing to her, he had thought he could take her away from the endless work that seemed to have been her lot in life. Now here she was slaving over something for his aunt, when—as his fiancée—she had no need to do it.

He couldn't deny she looked beautiful with her hair curtaining her face and her lithe fingers working their magic on what he recognized as one of the castle's vast collection of antique table linens. The pattern was a heritage rose design he had seen around him all his life, without paying it much attention. Now he noticed that the bloom on the embroidered roses matched the bloom on Meagan's cheeks as she concentrated.

He watched her, loath to disturb the picture she made. All she needed was a tall pointed hat and a satin gown spilling around her feet to look like an image from a tapestry herself. She made him feel like a knight in armor, he thought, liking the idea more than was good for him. Riding to her rescue had a lot of appeal. Sweeping her onto his horse and carrying her off had even more.

Too bad it wasn't going to happen. She had made it clear that she wanted their engagement to last only until the king was found and restored to the throne. Then he would have to release her. He sensed that, of all the challenges he'd faced in his life, this was going to be the most difficult. Sometimes he wished he wasn't a man of his word.

He wondered what she would say if she knew he loved her. She didn't want it, and he didn't want to feel it, but he hadn't a clue how to stop himself. The strength of the feeling scared the wits out of him. It was worse, much worse, than anything he'd felt before.

Watching her nimbly repair embroidered flowers with stitches you needed a magnifying glass to see, he felt a surge of warmth. A lock of hair fell across her eyes and she brushed it away impatiently. He didn't think he could bear to watch her much longer without taking her into his arms. They ached with emptiness.

He'd known he loved her from the moment he'd dragged her out of the line of fire during the raid. He'd threatened to handcuff her to a tree for her own good, then found himself on fire with the image that conjured up. Helpless, she wouldn't have been able to stop him ravaging her mouth until she was as aroused as she made him. Heck of a time for an erotic fantasy, but Meagan had that effect on him and more.

Telling himself he'd been angry with her for endangering herself didn't wash anymore. His anger went all the way back to Marina for getting killed and leaving him, he recognized at long last. He'd dispelled a lot of the anger during the raid, using more force than strictly necessary to demolish the cottage door. In the process, he'd felt something break loose for good. He was free of the anger now, too late to repair things between himself and Meagan.

He coughed to catch her attention. "Aunt Josephine said I'd find you in here. What are you doing?"

Meagan looked up, unable to stop herself flushing at the sight of him. "I'm helping to restore some antique embroideries," she said.

He frowned. "There are servants to do that."

"I love this work. It's what I'm trained to do. Molly's asleep, and I have no chores, so I want to do something useful."

He slid a hand under her chin, tilting her face up. "You don't have to be useful."

Lighting arced through her at his touch. "I can't sit around the castle all day, looking decorative."

"You can't help it."

She put aside the delicate fabric and fiddled with the tea-chest-sized box of threads provided for her when she'd agreed to undertake the work. At least the queen had understood Meagan's need to make a contribution of her own. On the previous afternoon, Queen Josephine had invited Meagan to take tea with her, and had quizzed Meagan on her professional background. Meagan's answers and a demonstration of her embroidery skills had impressed the queen sufficiently that she had offered Meagan the position of Curator of Antique Napery at the castle. She had a feeling now wasn't the time to tell Ben she had accepted. She needed the distraction of useful work, to help her deal with their sham engagement.

As a child, she had never expected to be grateful to her mother and elderly cousin for making her learn the old needleworking skills, but now she was. They would stand her in good stead when it came to preserving and restoring the valuable pieces collected in the castle over generations. "Cousin Maude didn't raise me to be idle," she said.

"Then it's time you learned the art." He took the fragile table runner out of her hands and set it aside.

She let her empty hands drift to her lap and lifted her chin. "Fortunately, the queen doesn't share your antiquated ideas about a woman's place. She's asked me to take over the care of the royal napery collection."

"You've agreed?" He read the answer in her expression, and his jaw tightened. "When were you going to ask for my opinion?"

She twisted a length of bright carmine thread between her fingers. "I suppose now you've announced our engagement, you're going to lecture me on how I should behave as a royal fiancée?"

A decanter of brandy sat on a side table. He went to it and poured a glass. "There's no need. I decided not to make the announcement."

She folded the table runner carefully between sheets of protective paper, then placed the bundle into a camphorwood box. Slowly, she closed the lid. She didn't want a sham engagement, so why did she feel as if the ground had fallen away beneath her?

There could be only one reason why Ben had chosen not to proceed with their mock engagement. "You've identified the traitor?"

He swirled the brandy in the glass but didn't drink. "Not yet, but Adam assures us it won't be long. If the traitor is close to the family, they already know I've sought the queen's blessing for our marriage, so there's nothing more to gain by going public."

"Less fanfare will also make it easier to end the charade as soon as the traitor is caught," she agreed.

He downed the drink in a quick swallow. "Isn't it what you want? You have the protection of being known as my fiancée within these walls, but you're still free to wait for Molly's father to reappear in your life."

"He isn't likely to, nor would I give him houseroom if he did," she snapped, too distraught by his decision to keep up the pretense any longer.

Ben put the glass down with exaggerated care. "You said you were in love with him."

"*You* said I was in love with him."

She heard his breath catch as he said, "You didn't correct my assumption."

Needing something to occupy her hands, she took an antimacassar out of the chest and spread it across her knees. The exquisite embroidery blurred before her eyes. "What's the point of going over this now?"

He took the cloth from her and set it aside, then grasped her hands, urging her to her feet. "First rule of piloting—make sure you're operating from correct information. Are you in love with Molly's father, Meagan?"

She turned her head away, unable to look at him but unable to lie, either. "He took advantage of my compassion to trick me into bed once, that was all. I never loved him. He left us before Molly was born. I have no idea where he is now."

Ben's hand slid under her chin, forcing her to meet his gaze. To her amazement, he didn't look angry. He looked—relieved, she thought, hardly able to believe it.

"Then you're truly free?"

"No."

His brow furrowed. "But you said…"

She touched a finger to his lips. "Hear me out. I can never be free because my heart belongs to a gallant man who doesn't want any woman's love."

Ben's features darkened. "He must be a fool."

"Never that. He had a bad experience that made him decide against loving again. He became overly protective of women, and he reacts badly when they object to being treated as dependents."

Understanding dawned and with it, a simmering anger that made her quail. "So what in blazes am I supposed to do? Stand by and watch you come to harm? My actions caused one woman's death. I'm not prepared to let it happen again."

"You didn't kill your fiancée," she said softly, wishing there was some way she could take away the anguish she saw in his gaze.

He gave a savage shake of his head. "If I hadn't decided to stand her down from the mission because she wasn't ready, she wouldn't have felt driven to take someone else's place and been killed."

"According to your old C.O., you were right, she wasn't ready."

"I could have kept my mouth shut."

"And she would have done precisely what she did do, one way or another. Mike Stafford is right when he says we have to be true to ourselves. You wouldn't have loved her if she'd been a brown mouse."

"Brown mice have their redeeming qualities."

"If you like brown mice." If he did, pity help her, because she didn't know how to be one.

He read her mind. "No one can accuse you of being a brown mouse."

She could hardly say the words, "Yet you want to mold me into one."

He hesitated, then his expression cleared. "I know I'll regret saying this, but I don't want you to change."

"Then stop blaming yourself for something that wasn't your responsibility. Otherwise it's going to keep coming between us forever. I don't think I could stand that."

He slid a heated palm down the side of her face. "I care about you, Meagan."

"And I care about you. I promise I'll take care of myself, but if there's to be a chance for us, I can't let you take over living for me. Don't you see, if we do that, the conspirators win, and we become prisoners ourselves, afraid in case they strike at those we love."

His fingers tangled in her hair. "You said your heart belongs to a man who doesn't want it. What would you say if you knew he wants it more than life itself?"

She pulled in a shuddering breath. "I'd wonder if this was another attempt to control my life."

"It would be difficult when his own is so far out of control, he's in a tailspin with the ground coming up fast."

She looked up and saw the confusion in his gaze, mirroring her own. "This is sudden, isn't it?"

His hands tightened around hers. "Define *sudden*."

She moistened dry lips. "Feeling as if your world will come to an end if you don't get the answer you want."

He nodded. "That's reasonably accurate."

"I know, because I feel the same way." She lowered her lashes to hide the depth of feeling she knew her eyes revealed, then lifted them again. "This isn't a ploy to get me to admit how much I need you, is it?"

"I thought I was the one doing the admitting."

"Seems to be mutual so far. Oh, Ben, I was afraid

if I let myself love you, you'd take over my life, and I couldn't allow it."

"And now?"

"Nothing seems to matter except being with you."

A slow smile dawned on his craggy features. "That I understand. I wish I could tell you I won't try to mollycoddle you in future, but it wouldn't be true. Even now, my instinct is to protect you from all that's bad in the world."

"I could get used to it, I suppose. This cloak-and-dagger stuff isn't really my style."

"You could have fooled me, barging into your house after you'd heard all those bullets."

"You were in there," she said simply.

He heard the truth in her voice, and his own became ragged with emotion. "You really love me that much?"

"More than I can put into words."

"Then we'll have to find some other way, because I feel the same about you."

He pulled her into his arms, kissing her so soundly that the room reeled around her. Light-headed, she kissed him back with a passion that left her breathless, loving the way he held her as if he never meant to let her go.

Her heart skipped a beat. Would it always be like this with him? Even as she argued her need for freedom, she surrendered it to him so willingly that she felt confused. Could she truly be free if it meant living without Ben?

She could hardly breathe for the sensations eddying through her. So this was how it felt to be swept off one's feet. She nuzzled his cheek, feeling the gentle abrasion of masculine skin against her feminine softness. "Are you sure you're not just saying you love me to get your own way?"

He nibbled her ear, spearing her with sensation all the way to her core. "It seems to be working."

"You don't know how well." She could hardly force the words out around a throat turned arid with desire. "Waiting until we're married is going to seem like a lifetime."

A groan slid from him. "For me, too. But we can't think of ourselves until King Michael is safely back on the throne."

"I know, but it's going to be so hard."

"Think of how wonderful it will be when we can finally be together, dearest Meagan."

He startled her by dropping to one knee beside her, keeping tight hold of both her hands. "Meagan Moore, will you do me the honor of becoming my wife?"

"You asked once before, and I accepted. Nothing has changed. But yes, I will marry you because I love you with all my heart."

He stood, gathering her against him. "Everything has changed. This time, our engagement is for real…and forever."

He'd said that he didn't believe in forever, but he said it now with such conviction that Meagan shivered. "It can't possibly get any better than this."

His eyes darkened with unmistakable passion as he feathered kisses along her brow line. "Oh yes, my darling, it can, and it will as soon as you are my wife. That's a promise."

An earthquake of needs and longings tore through her. She clung to him for support. He felt rock-steady, reassuring. He would always be her rock, she thought. As she would be his. "I've heard that the Duke of Norbourg always keeps his promises," she whispered.

He held her tightly against him. "Always, my darling duchess."

A commotion at the door made her spring away from him, although he kept his fingers entwined with hers. Molly rocketed into the room, followed more sedately by Queen Josephine.

She dismissed Meagan's graceful curtsy with a wave of her hand. "This adorable child wanted to see you."

Meagan ruffled Molly's hair. "Not as much as I want to see her."

"Queen Josephine took me to her special garden."

"I hope you haven't made a pest of yourself."

Queen Josephine shook her head. "The child is a tonic for me."

When she was with Molly, the queen could subdue her concern for King Michael at least for a while, Meagan thought, feeling satisfied at the good her child was doing.

"When the two of you are married, I hope Molly will come to regard me as an aunt," Josephine said, confirming the thought.

"When you marry my new daddy, will you have a real crown, and live happily ever after?" Molly asked.

Meagan's look found Ben. "I don't need a crown,

sweetheart. I already have all I need to live happily ever after."

Josephine inclined her head at Ben, her gaze softening. "She'll do."

Ben gathered Meagan into one arm and Molly into the other, his smile lighting up the room. "Just what I was thinking myself," he said.

Epilogue

Prince Edward Stanbury rose to his feet and lifted his glass. "I would wish for our dear brother, Michael, to perform this pleasant task, but I'm sure he wouldn't want me to delay on his account. So I propose a toast to Ben and his lovely bride-to-be, Meagan. Long life and happiness to you both."

The small group of royals joined Edward on their feet and raised their glasses. "To Ben and Meagan." Ben took her hand and squeezed it as the others resumed their seats.

He stood up. "Thank you all for your good wishes. I regret this must be a subdued gathering, but my dear aunt insisted that family morale would benefit if we came together to mark our engagement.

I can see it was a wise idea, as are all Queen Josephine's ideas."

The queen inclined her head graciously, but her eyes shone when she looked up again. "We were concerned that you might escape if Meagan didn't pin you down once and for all."

He gave a rueful smile, well aware that the queen had suspected his feelings for Meagan before Ben fully realized them himself. "No chance. I know when I'm well off," he said.

Meagan had also worried that it was unseemly to celebrate their engagement until the king was restored to his throne, but couldn't argue with the queen's logic. The family members did look happier than they had in a long while, she thought looking at the faces around the table. And now, thanks to a false leak by Royal Security that Prince Nicholas was supposedly dead, the Stanburys seemed hopeful that the kidnappers' identities would soon be revealed. It was a shame that Ben's father was away at sea and couldn't join them, but his mother, Princess Karenna, was there. Only the previous day, Ben had flown Meagan and Molly to his family home so they could meet the princess and bring her back to the castle for this occasion.

She had a mother again, Meagan thought, feeling a lump clog her throat. Princess Karenna had brushed aside Meagan's attempts at formality, assuring her that titles were never permitted to come between family members. The implication that she was already considered a member of the family brought tears of joy to Meagan's eyes.

The princess had welcomed Molly with special delight, saying that she was looking forward to being a grandmother at long last. Ben's answering frown showed that his mother's emphasis on the last words weren't lost on him. The warmth of the look he directed at Meagan also suggested that the princess wouldn't have to wait too long to become a grand-mother a second time.

Even Prince Nicholas had been smuggled into the castle under cover of darkness, although he had to return to his safe haven before sunrise. He looked pale and tense, but happy to be reunited with his family.

Seeing them together, Meagan was impressed by the resemblance between her fiancé and the prince. No wonder the conspirators had mistaken Ben for Nicholas. She never would, she knew. To her Ben was a man like no other. He possessed an unmistakable aura that set him apart. Meagan was prejudiced, of course. Watching him, relaxed for the moment as he took his seat and chatted with his cousin, she felt awed by the strength of a love that threatened to consume her.

"Never thought I'd see the day," Isabel said, resting her chin on one hand as she watched Ben.

"See what day?" Meagan asked.

"That Ben would be head over heels in love."

"It isn't the first time," Meagan pointed out with scrupulous fairness.

Isabel smiled. "Want to bet? He has loved before,

but never with this intensity. If the queen had withheld her blessing, he'd have propped a ladder at your window and carried you off anyway. Luckily she's as taken with you as the rest of us. We think you're just what Ben needs."

There had been times when she'd feared that the headstrong princess might not think her a suitable addition to the royal family, so Meagan appreciated the vote of confidence. "I know he's what I need," she said, meaning it with all her heart.

Isabel sighed. "Someday I might find out how that feels. But my love life must wait until we find my father."

"The list I gave you should provide some new leads."

Isabel dropped long lashes over her expressive eyes. "It will, but progress is frustratingly slow. I'm going to tell Adam that he and I should go undercover together to work our way through your list more quickly. You've obviously turned Ben's attitude around. He's not only agreed with my plan, he said he'll back me up when I take it to Adam Sinclair."

Meagan frowned. "Won't your plan be terribly dangerous?"

Isabel shrugged. "It may be the only way to get results. Until we identify the traitor within the castle, we dare not trust too many people."

"But you trust Adam. Does that mean—"

Isabel's gaze flashed fire. "Don't say it. It's bad enough to have the others matchmaking on my behalf, without you too."

Meagan admired the solitaire diamond Ben had

placed on her ring finger as a fiery symbol of their love. "Love has a lot to recommend it," she said huskily. "You should give it a try."

To her surprise, Isabel nodded. "After the king is restored to the throne, you never know your luck."

Meagan *did* know her luck, as she met Ben's heated gaze across the table. In it she read his impatience to be finished with the dinner so he could be alone with her. She wanted it too, but she schooled herself to patience. After the king was rescued, they would have all the time in the world to celebrate their love, with a fairy-tale castle as a setting.

Looking at her royal husband-to-be with his head bent as he listened intently to a story Molly was telling him, Meagan thought in fascination that, in their case, her child's favorite Sleeping Beauty story had been turned on its head. The sleeping prince had awoken under *Meagan's* care instead of the other way around, and not with a kiss, at least not at first. They had more than made up for lost time since then, she thought, feeling her face growing warm. Ben's kisses had the power to make her senses spin. As a lover he would be incomparable, and she felt her heartbeat quicken in anticipation.

She was elated that one fairy-tale tradition remained unchanged, at least. She and Ben *would* live happily ever after. Of that she had absolutely no doubt.

* * * * *

Fall in Love with...

MEN
in UNIFORM

MUBPA10

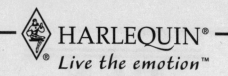

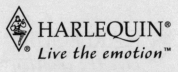

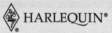

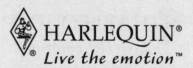

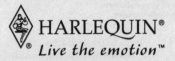

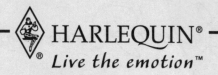